THE NOVELIZATION

THE NOVELIZATION

Adapted by Eric Geron

Based on *Descendants 2*, written by

Josann McGibbon & Sara Parriott

DISNEP PRESS

Los Angeles • New York

Printed in the United States of America
First Hardcover Edition, June 2017
1 3 5 7 9 10 8 6 4 2
FAC-020093-17125

Library of Congress Control Number: 2017934088

ISBN 978-1-4847-9970-3

For more Disney Press fun, visit www.disneybooks.com
Visit DisneyChannel.com

THIS LABEL APPLIES TO TEXT STOCK

To my fellow Villain Kids,
for following me to the Isle and back

CHAPTER ONE

MAL HERE. REMEMBER ME?

FOR THOSE WHO DON'T: I'M THE DAUGHTER OF THE WICKED SORCERESS MALEFICENT—BUT HEY, JUST 'CAUSE I'M THE SPAWN OF A VILE VILLAIN, IT DOESN'T MEAN I'M FOLLOWING IN MOM'S FIERY FOOTSTEPS. WELL, I GUESS *TINY* FOOTSTEPS IS MORE FITTING, BECAUSE MOM'S BEEN A LITTLE LIZARD EVER SINCE SHE WENT ALL FIRE-BREATHING DRAGON ON ME AND MY FRIENDS AND SHRANK TO THE SIZE OF THE LOVE IN HER HEART. IN CASE YOU MISSED THAT: NOT A LOT OF LOVE. BIG SHOCK. ME AND MY FRIENDS REALIZED THAT WE DIDN'T HAVE TO BE LIKE OUR VILLAIN PARENTS. WE CHOSE TO BE GOOD OVER EVIL (*ACTUAL* BIG SHOCK), AND KING BEN AND I HAD OUR HAPPILY EVER AFTER.

YOU DIDN'T THINK THAT WAS THE END OF THE STORY, DID YOU?

1

CHAPTER TWO

AURADON IS ALL BLUE SKIES AND BUTTERFLIES. I MEAN, WHAT COULD BE BETTER?

HOW ABOUT DREAMING UP ALL THE WAYS TO BE WICKED?

WHAT CAN I SAY? SOME THINGS NEVER CHANGE.

Mal and her friends stood around a large steaming cauldron in the dark.

She was wearing her signature tough-as-nails boots, ripped leggings, and leather jacket. Her dark purple hair was longer and thicker than ever before. She looked down at her hands, holding her mother's spell book, which she had spray-painted with acid-green and purple flames that caged the glinting gold dragon in the center. She glanced up at her three friends. There was something venomous in her smile.

Despite living in Auradon, Mal was still very much Maleficent's daughter.

Evie, daughter of Evil Queen, grinned at Mal. She wore a distressed blue leather jacket, a graffitied skirt, and a necklace with a red gem topped by a gold crown. Evie tossed back her silky blue hair as she stirred the steaming cauldron brew.

Jay, son of Jafar, held a bucket of shiny red apples. His biceps bulged out of his sleeveless red-and-yellow leather vest, and his long dark hair flowed from under a beanie. Jay emitted great strength and confidence. A light from the cauldron made his eyes sparkle danger- ously, and he gazed across the swirling mist at Carlos.

Carlos, son of Cruella De Vil, also held a bucket of shiny red apples. He was a skinny teen with spiky white hair with black roots, and he wore a red, white, and black fur-trimmed jacket. He looked at his three friends and snickered.

Mal smirked, opened the spell book, and read aloud: "'Wicked ways beneath the skin, let all who taste it now join in!'" She and her friends stared at the cauldron.

The brew began to spit, boil, and bubble. The spell had worked. Mal and her friends cackled triumphantly. Jay and Carlos dumped the apples into the thickening brew. The four Villain Kids (or VKs for short) circled the cauldron, howling, and refilled the buckets with the spelled apples. They were about to make mischief.

They knew all too well the many ways to be wicked.

Within minutes, Carlos was dumping a bucket of the spelled apples down the floor of the bright Auradon Prep hallway in front of the lockers. Cheerful students in yellow-and-blue tourney jerseys, cheerleading uniforms, and pastel-colored garments watched the apples roll past. They dove to snatch them. After biting into the wicked fruit, they whooped and danced in delight, instantly transformed from well-mannered to maniacal. Mal strutted over the apples, slamming the doors to lockers. The locker doors revealed the tag LONG LIVE EVIL!, which Mal had spray-painted there. She stopped in front of a shy girl wearing a large white bow in her chestnut hair.

It was Jane, daughter of Fairy Godmother. She gasped as Mal handed an apple to her. Stock-still, in her blue, white, and yellow cheerleading uniform, she stared at it. She chomped down on the apple, and her mouth twisted into a sinister grin. Jane snatched the spray paint can from Mal and boldly danced out of sight.

The apples had an intoxicating effect as Mal and her friends continued to share them across the sunny campus. They were making everyone—and every*thing*—a whole lot more fun. Outside, cheerleaders with apples did a routine with Jay before he ran off. In the school hall, Carlos slid into a group of guys, who fell over. One student bit into an apple, then screwed his hat on backward and did a flip off the lockers. In one of the classrooms, Evie strolled through rows of students and doled out apples. She strutted to Fairy Godmother's desk, placed an apple on it, and moved on. Fairy Godmother, the school's headmistress, bit into the apple. She looked up and saw that chaos had erupted: Evie and the students danced and threw loose papers into the air. Fairy Godmother shimmied and shook out her hair, joining in the madness that had seized her once neat and orderly classroom.

The wicked fever kept on spreading.

On the quad, Jay chucked apples off the balcony with glee. Doug, son of Dopey, was playing the trumpet when one of Jay's apples landed in it. More apples dropped into the trumpets of other band members, as well. As Jay continued to fire the apples rapidly, the band players scrambled to catch them and chomp down.

In the rose garden, students kneeled around the stone fountain and dunked their faces into the clear water. One by one, they emerged, flipping back their wet hair with glistening apples in their mouths. Everyone wanted a bite of true evil and mad mischief. They couldn't get enough. Other students who overlooked the busy lawns jumped up and down, waved their apples, and danced victoriously.

Mal, Evie, Jay, and Carlos reunited as a fierce squad at the front of Auradon Prep—the castle-like building with proud blue-and-gold banners rustling from the stone battlements. They rallied the dancing students. Among them were Beast and Belle, who also clutched bitten apples and jived to the sound of wicked rebellion.

Mal marched through a row of hedges and raised into the air the school flag, which was now a dark purple one that said LONG LIVE EVIL! The horde cheered. Mal loved it. She led everyone farther away from the school, climbed a ladder, and spray-painted the fearsome statue that represented King Ben's father in beast form.

Mal recalled something her boyfriend, Ben, had once said about the statue: *My father wanted his statue to morph from beast to man to remind us that anything is possible.* Anything was possible, indeed. Mal could laugh at the irony.

She grinned and tossed the last one of the spelled apples high into the air.

It came down, and King Ben, golden boy and only child of Belle and Beast, caught it. He flashed Mal an innocent smile, and his eyes sparkled angelically beneath honey-brown hair that swooped across his forehead. Ben hadn't been changed—not yet. He bit into the apple and a devilish grin broke over his face.

HA!
IF ONLY.

CHAPTER THREE

FINE. THAT NEVER HAPPENED. BUT A GIRL CAN DREAM, RIGHT? THIS IS HOW THE STORY *ACTUALLY* PICKS UP. . . .

Flashing cameras snapped Mal back to reality.

Like *that*, she was no longer leading all of Auradon Prep in a rotten-to-the-core victory march. Instead, Mal faced a mass of rowdy news reporters and camerapeople at a press conference. Her signature leather getup and long purple hair were no more. In fact, Mal looked every bit a prissy princess, like the very ones she used to mock when she lived on the Isle of the Lost, except that instead of pretty in pink, Mal's lace dress was white, and her hair was ice blond and pinned up in a bun. There was a slight purple ombré to the tips—the only trace left of her villain roots.

"Mal!" the news reporters called out, shoving microphones in her face.

Mal remembered to breathe, and to smile. *Be ladylike,* she reminded herself.

"Only three days to the Royal Cotillion!" shouted a reporter.

"Ever think a girl like you would be lady of the court?" yelled another.

Mal turned from face to face, unsure of which to address first.

"How do you feel being the most *envied* girl in Auradon?"

"Do you like being a blonde?"

"Is your mother *still* a lizard?"

Mal opened her mouth. She was unable to formulate a single word.

"Okay! All right!" said Ben to the camera crew as he leaped to Mal's side, looking dashing in his royal-blue suit. He held an ordinary apple with a bite taken out of it. "We will let you know *if* and *when* that particular situation changes," he told reporters.

Mal felt momentarily relieved, but the reporters resumed shouting.

"King Ben, did you ever think you'd be with a Villain Kid?"

"We're done here," Ben said to the crowd, doing his best to ignore the ruckus. He faced Mal and smiled kindly.

Fairy Godmother tottered through the rose garden and stepped between Mal and Ben and the frenzied crowd. Her hair was up in a loose bun, and she wore pearl earrings and a lavender dress with a big pink bow at the neck, as always. She addressed the raucous mass. "Okay, okay," she said. "Shoosh, shoosh, shoosh, shoosh, shoosh." She motioned for silence with her hands. "This is still a school. So if you're here, you're either skipping or trespassing! Either way, I need you to—"

People began to spout remarks.

"Shhh! Shhh! Shhhhhh!" said Fairy Godmother, gesturing again for silence. Once the crowd finally quieted, she smiled. "Shhh!" she added with a merry little laugh.

The news reporters began to disperse.

For good measure, Fairy Godmother said, "Shhh! Shhh! Shhh! Shoo."

Before long, almost the whole crowd had receded to the edge of the lawn.

"Thank you. Thank you so much. Thank you," called Fairy Godmother.

"Thank you, guys!" said Ben with a wave.

"Thank you!" said Mal—and she meant it.

"Mal. Ben," said Fairy Godmother with a nod of acknowledgement.

"Fairy Godmother," replied Mal and Ben in unison.

Fairy Godmother's work was done. She turned and scampered off.

Mal looked at Ben. "Hi," she said, letting out a flustered laugh.

Ben beamed a comforting smile. "Just ignore them," he said of the throng of reporters, who were now milling at a safe distance with their cameras at their sides.

"That's a *lot* easier said than done." Mal gave him a slight smile.

Ben pulled Mal close to him. "I know, I know. Maybe we should go out. . . . We should—" He glanced at his golden watch. "*Oh my God. I am so* late for a council meeting!" He looked into Mal's green eyes and winced. "I have got to go!" he said.

"That's okay." Mal had nothing but understanding in her voice.

"We'll finish this, though, okay?" said Ben sincerely.

"Yeah," said Mal, nodding. In a way, she was strangely relieved.

More time to rest, she thought. *Keeping up this act is exhausting.*

Evie ran up behind Mal. Stylish as always, she wore a blue dress with a gold collar and belt. Her long blue hair was down in loose waves, held in place by a delicate gold headband encrusted with red gems. Evie grabbed Mal's arm and spun her around. Mal cried out in surprise.

"If we don't do a fitting for your gown right this minute, you'll be dancing in your bathrobe," Evie told Mal. "Bye, Ben," she added as she deftly dragged Mal away.

There goes my nap. Mal turned back to Ben and mouthed, *Bye, Ben.*

In a flash, the news reporters swarmed Ben

with microphones and cameras aimed like swords. "King Ben! King Ben! Just one question about the cotillion—"

Ben glanced at his watch again. "I've really got to go." He speed-walked away.

The noisy news reporters followed right behind him.

CHAPTER FOUR

I'M FAR FROM BEING A PERFECT LADY OF THE COURT.
IT'S ONLY A MATTER OF TIME BEFORE PEOPLE SEE
RIGHT THROUGH ME.

Sunlight shone through the polished windows into
Mal and Evie's dorm.

Evie had made herself at home. A bejeweled peri-
odic table of the elements dominated a wall, and
her worktable hosted spools of fabric, her sewing
machine, an assortment of multisize boxes, colored
pencils, and pages of clothing designs she had drawn.
Beside the worktable, Evie's handmade dresses hung
on a rack. One look at Evie's side of the room and it
was clear fashion designing was her passion.

Mal's half of the room was much more of a zoo.
The lizard in an aquarium tank on Mal's bedside

table didn't help matters. It bore a sign that said DON'T FEED MY MOM, for inside was none other than the evil Maleficent, who had been transformed at King Ben's coronation ceremony from a giant powerful dragon to a puny green lizard. As the lizard sat on the mini-throne inside her aquarium, Mal stood on a fitting platform so Evie could fit her cotillion gown.

The blue-and-yellow garment, with its layers of tulle and darkly glinting gems, was crafted for a true queen. Evie yanked the dress tight in the bodice and pinned it.

Mal squawked. "Evie. I cannot breathe."

Evie lifted Mal's arm. "Well, you can breathe after Cotillion." She smiled.

Mal let out a sarcastic laugh. "Yeah, well, I sincerely doubt that. I have like twenty more events directly behind it, and I can't even remember what a single one of them is right now." Mal looked longingly at her leather Isle of the Lost jacket, hanging on a hook above the TV. She thought about when she had been rotten to the core—with her purple hair and jacket—and feared and respected by everyone on the Isle.

"Evie," Mal said in a distant way.

"Huh?" Evie held a measuring tape across Mal's gown.

"Do you ever wonder what we'd be doing right now if we were still back on the Isle?" asked Mal. Her mind floated to her friends' hideout there, where they had spent time plotting and planning, crafting mischievous schemes to cause serious trouble.

Evie laughed, not really paying attention to Mal's question. "That's funny," she said, turning. "Well, would ya look at who's on TV!" She grabbed the remote, cranked up the volume, and listened to the television while studying some of her sketches.

Behind her, Mal plopped down in a sea of yellow tulle onto her canopy bed.

She and Evie watched an old clip playing on the screen. In it, Mal was sporting a beaded sheer dress with a shawl and a delicate gold headpiece. Aladdin, in a cream-colored suit and hat, and Jasmine, in a long sheer turquoise dress, greeted Mal and King Ben. Servers placed a meal in the center of a room filled with cushions and candles. Aladdin escorted Mal to her seat while Ben led Jasmine to hers. Aladdin and

Ben sat down across from each other, and a waitress uncovered a silver dish.

Mal picked up a piece of meat. She bit into it and gagged but covered it up with a quick smile. When no one was looking, Mal spit it out into a napkin, which she stashed behind her, and beamed at her company. Watching the TV, Mal blanched.

"Six months ago, no one thought King Ben and his girl from the wrong side of the bridge would last," said a news reporter.

"Yeah, no kidding," Mal mumbled.

The news reporter continued. "I don't know her secret, but Mal is fitting in *beautifully* now!" Footage played of Mal at the press conference earlier that day. She smiled and waved with her white lace gloves. "Mal must be counting down the days till the Royal Cotillion, where she will officially become a lady of the court."

Mal's eyes opened wide. *Don't remind me,* she thought. She scooted around her bed and took the etiquette book *The Lady's Manners* from her bedside table. Then she pulled her spell book from under her pillow, opened it, and incanted: *"Read it fast, at lightning speed, remember everything I need."* She quickly turned the pages of *The Lady's Manners* and was able to magically absorb the book's facts.

Evie walked over to Mal. "Well, *I* know Mal's secret to fitting in, and Ben wouldn't like it one bit." She crossed her arms. "Haven't you guys had enough secrets between the two of you?"

Mal looked up from *The Lady's Manners.* "You saw what I was like before I started using the spell book, okay?" she said. "I was a complete *disaster!*" She resumed flipping through the pages of the book.

"Well, personally, as your best friend, I strongly believe you should put this spell book in the museum along with my mirror," said Evie. She was referring to the magic mirror Evil Queen had once given her so she could find and steal Fairy Godmother's wand. Evie had turned over a new leaf. No more wickedness. She grabbed Mal's spell book, and Mal pouted at Evie and then shut *The Lady's Manners.* "Don't give me the face," said Evie. "Put the pout away."

Mal frowned.

"You know I'm right," added Evie.

"Don't you ever miss just running wild and breaking all the rules?" Mal asked.

Evie grinned. "Like stealing, lying, and fighting?"

Mal smiled dreamily at Evie's words. "Yeah!"

Evie's grin faded. *"No!"* she shouted, breaking Mal out of her fantasy.

"What—" Mal started.

"Why would we?" Evie laughed. "M, come here!" She took Mal's hands and led her off the bed and toward the TV. "Look at where we are! We're in *Auradon*! And we're Auradon girls now." Evie gazed at the screen, and her face broke into a smile.

A video showed Mal, dressed in a crystal-encrusted gown, with Ben, who wore a smart suit. They were seated at a table, covered by a white tablecloth, with strawberries in a dish and steaming cups of coffee. Ben fed a chocolate-covered strawberry to Mal. She then took a strawberry in her white-lace-gloved hand, dunked it into the molten chocolate, and fed it to Ben. She got chocolate on his face and helped him wipe it off, laughing happily. Ben dipped another strawberry in the chocolate and fed it to her.

Mal took a bite, nodded dreamily, and nestled her head in the crook of Ben's neck.

"And of course, there's Mal's *wardrobe!*" exclaimed the news reporter. "Auradon has never seen such a fresh, exciting look. Our hottest new designer, Evie, just keeps surprising us!"

"*See? This* is the land of opportunity!" Evie faced Mal. "We can be whatever we want to be here! So please, let's just leave the past in the past, okay? Besides, have you seen the shoes?" Evie lifted a pair of blue-and-gold high-heeled shoes off her worktable. "I mean, can we talk about the shoes?"

"Those are severe." Mal forced a little laugh.

The truth was Mal wasn't ready to leave her past behind. And she had never felt more distant from her best friend than she did at that moment.

CHAPTER FIVE

A S MOM USED TO SAY, FAKE IT TILL YOU MAKE IT.
(WELL, ACTUALLY SHE USED TO SAY, *"NURSE* IT TILL
YOU *CURSE* IT," BUT SAME THING.)

Between classes, Mal, Evie, Jay, and Carlos strolled outside the school.

Mal wore a frilly pale green dress, with her hair in long blond tendrils, and she clutched a textbook from Fairies 101. She kept her head down and walked beside Evie, who was the epitome of fashion in her blue dress and blue box purse, both of her own making. Jay and Carlos led Dude, Carlos's scruffy but adorable dog, on a leash. The friends climbed up steps onto a breezy open outdoor patio.

Fellow students, holding textbooks, were milling

about, perching in the niches of the school's stone wall, or sitting on a stone railing. They smiled at Mal and her friends. The VKs had come a long way since they had arrived in Auradon. They used to be looked down on for being the kids of terrible villains, but now the four were treated with respect. It helped that Mal was gearing up to be the lady of the court.

Jay nodded and pointed at a group of girls, who swooned.

"Why do you torture them?" Carlos asked. "Just pick someone to take to Cotillion already."

"I'm going solo. That way, I can dance with all of them." Jay squeezed Carlos's shoulder and grinned, waggling his eyebrows.

"Ah, you're the expert," said Carlos. "Let's say that you were going to ask someone. . . . What's the best way to go?"

"Listen." Jay rested his hand on Carlos's shoulder. "All you got to do . . . is look like me." Jay howled with laughter.

"Oh, ha-ha." Carlos rolled his eyes.

Evie chuckled, but Mal seemed lost in thought.

"Mal!" said Jane.

Mal snapped to attention.

Jane had appeared before Mal and her friends, clutching a tablet. Lonnie, daughter of Mulan, stood by her side, looking as chipper as ever. Lonnie's long black hair stood out against her bright pink dress.

But Mal was in no mood to answer more Cotillion questions from Jane, who was helping plan the event.

Carlos unwittingly distracted Jane. "Hey, Jane," he said nervously.

"Hey," said Jane, smiling at him.

"Uh, I was wondering . . . if you . . . uh . . . liked the carrot cake last night," he said.

"I had the pumpkin pie," she said sweetly, a bit confused.

"Oh. Cool." Carlos stared at her, unsure of what to say next to impress her.

Jay walked up behind him and gripped his shoulders. "Smooth," he said in a low voice. Then he swiftly dragged Carlos and Dude away to their next class.

Mal braced herself for the barrage of questions. Lucky for her, Evie chimed in.

"I have an opening for a fitting at three! Who wants it?" Evie asked the girls.

"Me!" Lonnie leaped in front of Jane, then winced. "Sorry," she added.

"Okay, so I'll see you later," Evie told Jane as she pulled Lonnie to the side to chat.

Mal was alone with Jane. She felt like a deer in headlights.

And Jane wasn't slowing down. "Mal! I hate to keep bugging you, but the Cotillion decorating committee needs more answers. So as much as I hate to . . . uh . . . to . . . uh—"

"Bug me," said Mal.

"Right." Jane nodded.

"Yeah. Uh, no. Totally. I—I just have to get to class." Mal jerked her thumb.

"You know what? Just nod if you like it." Jane held up her tablet.

"Okay," said Mal.

Jane used her stylus to sweep through an array of photos on the screen, one after another in a dizzying flurry. "Chair swags. Entry banner. Twinkle lights.

Uh, let's see. Napkin design. Table bunting . . ." Jane scrolled through even more photos.

Mal bobbed her head at each image.

"And you still haven't picked the party favors yet," Jane added.

"Jane, whatever you want to go with, I totally trust you—"

"I mean, we could do chains, key charms, pen toppers," interrupted Jane, continuing to tap through images. "I kind of love the pen toppers," she blurted out.

This was making Mal so anxious she could barely breathe.

"I mean, we could do all three if you want to . . ." continued Jane.

"You know—" Mal's eyes suddenly flashed bright green. Then she took a breath, and her eyes returned to their normal shade of green. She smiled and rested a hand gently on Jane's arm. "Pen toppers," she said.

"Uh-huh?" asked Jane.

"Yeah," said Mal. "Yeah."

"Okay! You won't regret it!" Jane beamed.

Evie and Lonnie walked back over to Jane and Mal.

"I can hardly wait to see what your wedding will look like!" Lonnie exclaimed.

"Oh yeah, me too," said Mal with a vacant smile. She froze then, realizing what Lonnie had said. "Wait, *what*?"

"Yeah!" said Jane. "The Royal Cotillion is like getting engaged to be engaged to be engaged!"

"I knew it!" Evie clasped her hands together, delighted.

"Everyone knows it," said Lonnie.

Mal's eyes bugged out. "*I* didn't know it!" she said. "How come nobody told me that? Is my entire life just planned out in front of me and no one was—"

Ben appeared at Mal's side in his royal-blue suit. "Hi, Mal!"

"Hiiii, Ben," Evie, Jane, and Lonnie said in singsong unison.

Mal glared at them. The whole engagement conversation had put her in an even worse mood.

Ben smiled, then moved to give Mal a kiss hello.

Jane grabbed him. "Oh, a quick moment!" She pulled Ben to the side.

Mal watched from a distance, then inched away.

"All right, the surprise is almost finished for Mal's big night," Jane told him once they were out of earshot. She held her tablet in front of him and showed him images of a stained glass window that had a young couple on it.

"Make sure her eyes are green," Ben told Jane.

Behind Jane, Mal caught Ben's attention and nodded sideways as if to say, *Are you coming with me?*

Ben called out to Mal that he'd catch up with her later before he turned his attention back to Jane.

"Which green should they use?" Jane asked. She showed a few rectangular pieces of green stained glass to Ben. The shades of green were all very similar.

"Uh . . ." Ben took them and smiled. He picked the darkest green. "This one." He stared through it dreamily, clearly picturing his gift for Mal.

In the girls' dorm room, Evie pinned the hem of Chad's faux-fur-trimmed cape.

Chad Charming, the pampered son of Cinderella, admired himself in the tall mirror, from his shiny shoes to the top of his sandy hair. "Oooh! What about peacock feathers?" Chad asked. "I betcha nobody's going to have *those* at Cotillion!"

Evie cleared her throat and let go of the hem. "You know what, Chad? When I look at you, all I can think of is . . . *king*." She framed him with her hands as if capturing greatness, then stole a furtive glance at Doug, who sat at Evie's worktable.

Doug, who looked every part the accountant in his owlish glasses, green bow tie, and long suspenders, had been tracking Evie's fashion design business on his computer, tallying numbers. He swiveled around in his chair and winked at Evie.

Oblivious, Chad gasped and grinned at Evie's words.

"And fake fur . . . Fake fur says it all," Evie told Chad, shaking the cape's trim.

Chad caressed the fake fur.

"Loud and clear," said Doug with a nod and a smile.

Jay popped into the room for a second to shout, "In the amphitheater in five!"

"Amphitheater in five," Chad said, mocking him. "Why did the coach make him captain instead of me? I'm *obviously* the better player." He struck an arrogant pose and grinned. *"King Chad,* though. Don't mind the sound of that. . . . You know who else would like that?"

"Who?" asked Evie, feigning interest.

"Audrey," said Chad.

"Hmmm, she would," said Evie, playing along.

"Chad!" Jay yelled. "Let's go!"

Chad frowned. "I'm coming!" He stepped off the fitting platform and made his way out of the room.

Evie carefully removed Chad's cape as he exited. Then she dropped it on the fitting platform and walked up to Doug. They looked at each other and broke into laughter.

"Not a lot of *there* there," they said in unison. Then they laughed again. Doug had said the same line to Evie about Chad when she had first shown interest in being Chad's girlfriend much earlier. Her crush on Chad hadn't lasted long: it turned out that vain and selfish guys weren't Evie's type. She was much more into the sweet and dapper Doug.

"Someone's obviously having some *serious* trouble dealing with his breakup with Audrey," Evie commented as she picked up a sketch showing a new dress with an intricate gold collar and belt.

Doug squinted his pale green eyes and peered through his glasses at his computer. "Hey, I've been doing the numbers." He began to type rapidly.

"Yeah?" Evie marked up her dress design with a pencil.

"And after we collect from all the girls for their gowns and Chad's cape . . ." Doug hit a few buttons.

"Uh-huh?" Evie set her paper down on the worktable and looked at Doug's computer screen. Her jaw dropped at the number she saw, and she laughed. "No wonder people *work*! Wow . . ." She looked up at Doug. "What am I going to do with all that money?" She looked back at the computer.

Doug tapped a few keys.

"In a few years, you could buy that castle you've

always wanted." He looked at Evie with utmost earnestness. "That way, you wouldn't need a prince."

Evie took his hand and gazed into his eyes. "You're right. I don't. Because I have you."

Evie loved her life in Auradon. It was everything she'd ever dreamed of.

CHAPTER SIX

UGH! I'M SO OVER THIS PLACE. AND APPARENTLY COTILLION IS A WAY BIGGER DEAL THAN I THOUGHT. GREAT. NOW I REALLY HAVE TO KEEP UP THE PERFECT PRINCESS ACT. CAN'T HAVE SOME ISLE HOOLIGAN RUINING BEN'S BIG DAY!

Mal raced to her locker, grabbed her purse from inside it, and rooted around in the bag.

"Hi, Mal," came a voice from beside her.

Mal staggered back and found Ben leaning against her locker door.

"Hi!" she said, trying to act cool. She let out a nervous laugh.

Ben smiled warmly at her. "I . . . have a little surprise for you."

Mal grinned. "Another one. Wow, that's, like, every day now."

"Every *other* day," said Ben, correcting her. "The even dates. Because you're *even* more perfect than I thought."

"That's me. I am perfect." She kept herself from rolling her eyes.

"Come on, let me spoil you," said Ben. "You know, you didn't have a lot growing up."

Mal's smile twitched. "We managed," she said.

Ben peered inside Mal's locker and saw her spell book sitting in a wire tray against the back. He pointed at the book. "Didn't you donate that to the museum?" He reached for it, but Mal guided his hand away, closed the locker door, and smiled.

"Is that still in there?" said Mal playfully. She brushed Ben's hair out of his eyes with her finger. "Um . . . I have to get to class. I do not want to be late, so—"

"No you don't," said Ben. "But . . ." He took Mal's hand and led her by the arm.

A few steps away, there was a sparkly purple motor scooter with a gold bow on top.

"Ta-da," said Ben, gesturing to it.

Mal gasped and cupped her hands to her mouth. *"What?"*

"Do you like it?" asked Ben.

Mal beamed, genuinely thrilled. "Does an *ogre* like *cheese puffs?*" She stepped closer to the scooter and inspected it, feeling the new seat and handles. "Ben! This is amazing!" She looked up at his smiling face. "I love it!" she said, examining the scooter again. She let out a joyful laugh. But then her face fell. "I haven't gotten you anything," she said, gazing at Ben.

"Oh, well, you're making me a picnic with all my favorite foods, remember?" Ben leaned back against the lockers and smiled.

"No, that's on Thursday," said Mal, patting Ben's chest reassuringly.

"It *is* Thursday," said Ben, reaching into his royal-blue jacket.

Mal laughed. "No it's not," she said. She grabbed for her purse.

Ben quickly pulled his phone out of his jacket pocket and showed the date to Mal. "Thursday," he said, confirming what Mal had hoped wasn't true.

Another slipup, Mal thought. *Great.* She sighed.

"But it's okay, you know—" Ben started.

"No, no, no, no. I knew it was Thursday, I was messing around." Mal laughed again. "I actually . . . I just have a few more things to finish cooking, and then I'm all yours! So I'm gonna go do that. It's all good. I'm good." Mal smiled like she truly meant it.

"What about class?" asked Ben.

"She multitasks!" Mal said, grinning. She patted Ben's chest affectionately and ran off.

"She dabbles!" Ben called after her.

Mal broke out into laughter.

"You're the best!" Ben shouted.

"That's me!" sang Mal.

But Mal couldn't help feeling that the opposite was true.

As captain of the R.O.A.R. team, Jay led practice in the amphitheater.

When tourney was having its off-season, some athletes at Auradon Prep took up all-new blue-and-gold uniforms boasting the school's crest to play R.O.A.R. They held lightweight swords, wore mesh masks that hid their faces, and sparred within the confines of an indoor arena. That day, students watched from behind a rail and from balconies as Jay and Carlos sparred with other masked opponents. Some team members jumped on blue-and-yellow concrete boxes evenly spaced around the perimeter of the arena to gain height. Chad looked on from the sidelines, motioning with his sword to try to match Jay's agile moves.

"Eyes on your opponent!" Jay shouted, demonstrating. "Light on your feet!"

Jay fought each of his opponents, forcing them to move out of bounds, where they removed their masks and watched from the sidelines as he faced his remaining competitor, who thrust a sword at Jay, challenging him. Jay removed his mask.

"Get him, Jay!" shouted Chad.

The masked fencer and Jay fought, sword striking sword.

It was an even match.

"Watch out, Jay!" said Carlos.

Jay and his adversary squared off again, sizing each other up.

Then they were back at it.

"C'mon, Jay!" Carlos called.

The masked figure spun, ripping Jay's sword from his hand.

Jay gasped.

The figure battled Jay backward to the rim of the arena.

Jay kicked his opponent's hand, sending his sword flying back into his own hand.

"Finish him!" shouted Chad.

But before either Jay or his opponent could make another agile move, the mystery fencer pulled off the headgear in surrender. A mane of shiny smooth black hair cascaded out. It was none other than Lonnie! Jay grinned at the revelation, impressed.

"Not bad!" said Chad as all the students applauded.

"You should put me on the team!" said Lonnie with a smile.

Chad stepped into the arena in front of her.

"What?" He looked at Jay. "No, dude, we'd be the laughingstock of the league, right, guys?" sputtered Chad. "I mean, what's gonna happen next, we're gonna have girls playing *tourney*?" Chad smirked.

"So?" Jay asked him.

Chad scoffed. "*So?* So, have you not read the rule book? Let me do that for ya." He fished the R.O.A.R. rule book out of his back pocket. "Section two, paragraph three-eleven-*dash*-four," he said, opening the book. " 'A team shall be comprised of a captain and eight *men*'!" read Chad. He held the book in the air, turned in a circle for the other students to see, and lowered it in front of Jay's face.

Jay pushed Chad's hand away.

"But you're down a man, since Ben had to leave to do all that king stuff," said Lonnie, annoyed at the silly rule and at Chad for enforcing it.

Chad let out an exasperated sigh. "Exactly. Down a *man*," he said, cocking his head to the side and pursing his lips in defiance.

"Jay," Lonnie said, hoping he had better news.

Jay looked at the floor, then shook his head,

genuinely unhappy. "I'm sorry," Jay told her. "Coach trusted me, and I'm not going to stay captain if I just throw out the rule book."

Lonnie stared long and hard at Jay, disappointed. "If my *mother* thought that way, she would have lost the war."

Chad sneered. *"Okay,"* he said in a mocking tone.

Lonnie sighed and started to walk away.

"Read the rule book," said Chad, shaking it at her back.

Jay sighed. "All right, guys. Let's call it. That's practice." He and his team filed out of the room.

On his way out, Carlos gazed up and saw Jane leaning on the balcony. She was in her cheerleading uniform and held her tablet. "Jane!" Carlos shouted. "Hey," he added.

"Hey, Carlos, what's up?" Jane smiled and looked down from the balcony.

Carlos hopped up onto a concrete block below her. "Uh . . . not much. You?"

Jane glanced at her tablet. "Way too much. We were going to go with the blue-and-gold banners for

Cotillion, but now we can't find the right shade of blue."

Dude, in his R.O.A.R. uniform, sat on a block and whined at Carlos.

"Uh . . . yeah . . . That's a bummer. . . . Uh, speaking of Cotillion—" said Carlos.

"I know, right?" Jane interrupted. "It's all anybody is talking about twenty-four seven. It's like they've never been to one before." Jane let out an annoyed laugh.

"Uh . . . I haven't," admitted Carlos quietly.

Jane's eyes opened wide. "Oh . . ." She quickly tried to save face. "Lucky," she said, shaking her head. "I always end up serving punch with my mom anyway. And this year I got stuck on the decorating committee, because Audrey went off to a *spa vacation* with Flora, Fauna, and Merryweather." Jane grimaced at the thought.

"Oh, uh . . . Hey! Maybe we should just, uh, you know . . ." Carlos blanched.

"Skip the whole thing? I really, really wish I could. . . . It's so nice to have a friend who's on the same wavelength." Jane beamed at him. Just then, her phone dinged, and she groaned. "I gotta go! Good practice, though!" Jane dashed off.

Dude looked at Carlos and whimpered. "It wasn't the right time, all right?" Carlos responded, exasperated.

CHAPTER SEVEN

FAKE IT TILL YOU MAKE IT? MORE LIKE FAKE IT TILL YOU *BREAK* IT!

I DON'T KNOW HOW MUCH LONGER I CAN PULL OFF THIS CHARADE BEFORE I COMPLETELY SNAP!

In the boys' dorm room, Carlos sat on his bed with his laptop and Dude.

"All right." Carlos let out a sigh. "How to get out of the friend zone," he murmured as he typed the phrase on the laptop.

From a plaid dog bed next to Carlos, Dude studied the screen.

Carlos pretended to glare at him. "I see you reading over my shoulder."

Dude blinked at him.

Mal burst into the room, shut the door, and locked it. She was panting. She paced back and forth, then saw the TV playing. There was a clip of Ben feeding strawberries to Mal. She rushed across the room and shut off the TV. Mal's whole body was quivering.

Her eyes flashed a dazzling green and a gust of magical power stirred her hair.

"Whoa, whoa. Easy, girl," Carlos remarked.

"What, you think this is so easy?" Mal walked around his bed and faced him. "You don't have people taking pictures of you every single time you open your mouth to say *boo*, not that I can even say *boo*, but ya know. . . ." Mal took a few deep breaths, and Carlos looked down and continued quietly typing on his laptop.

"Carlos," said Mal, throwing her hands up.

He looked up. "Yeah," he said absentmindedly.

"Do you ever miss screaming at people and making them run away from you?" asked Mal, hoping that someone other than her was missing the Isle.

"You're thinking of my mother, and I was usually on the other side of it. So not really, no," said Carlos. Then he bolted up. "Oh, hey, Mal. Did you bring it?"

As Mal raised something in her hand to show Carlos, someone rattled the doorknob. A second later, a key turned in the lock and the door opened. Chad crept in. When he saw Mal and Carlos, he froze.

"Oh! Hi!" he said with his classic cheesy fake smile. "Just came to use your 3-D printer. Won't be a sec," he said.

Carlos gawked. "How'd you get a key to my room?"

"Oh! I printed it up *last time* I was in here," said Chad nonchalantly. "You guys were sleeping." Chad strolled to the 3-D printer and turned it on. "Come on! Your printer is *so* much better than mine," he said. "And you installed all those hacks—"

"Out! Now!" Carlos pointed to the door, adding, "Leave the key."

"Fine." Chad dramatically left the room.

Carlos turned away from the door toward Mal. "Oh. Uh . . . my potion?" he asked.

Mal lifted a cherry-red gumdrop in her fingers. "Yeah. Um . . . here you go."

Carlos's face lit up. "So it'll make me say what I really feel to Jane?" he asked.

"I mean, it's a truth gummy, so take it or leave it," said Mal flatly.

"Awesome." Carlos reached out to grab it.

Mal hid it behind her back. "Hold on. No."

"What?" asked Carlos.

"Do you *really* wanna take this? Like, *always* telling the truth? I only ask because if I took this right now, I would get myself kicked back to the Isle. Not that that sounds ridiculously unappealing, but—"

"Yeah . . . Yeah, I'll take my chances." Carlos reached out his hand.

But before they knew it, Dude had leaped down and eaten the gumdrop from Mal's hand.

Mal gasped. "Bad dog!"

Dude jumped back onto the bed. "That thing was *nasty*," he said. "And *you*"—he spoke to Carlos—"you just gotta man up. And, while you're at it, scratch my butt."

Carlos and Mal stared at Dude in amazement.

"Well . . . you heard him," Mal told Carlos. "Scratch his butt."

Mal left the two of them to talk.

She had bigger fish to fry.

CHAPTER EIGHT

SPEAKING OF FISH, BEHIND THE MAGICAL BARRIER KEEPING ALL THE BADDIES ON THE ISLE OF THE LOST, EVIL WAS AFOOT IN ITS GREASIEST, FISHIEST, DARE I SAY, *SHRIMPIEST* FORM. . . .

Ursula's Fish and Chips sat on a dreary wharf on the Isle of the Lost.

A swashbuckling young man, Harry, son of Captain Hook, strolled toward the shop, holding a glinting silver hook in one hand. He wore a black pirate hat, a long red leather coat, black pants, and a smirk on his face that made other pirates quake. His piercing green eyes and sharp cheekbones made him both beautiful and frightening.

Harry passed through a dusty lane where bedraggled pirates were selling their gaudy wares. The dirty pirates regarded him with fear, leaping aside, huddling together, hiding, shaking, and watching him with wide eyes as he walked by.

Harry smiled to himself. He loved the attention.

He crossed a dock with frayed coils of rope and cracked crab traps on either side. His footsteps sounded heavily on the wood, drawing the attention of pirates lounging on barrels and surrounding platforms. He stopped in front of a rotten storefront. A plaque reading URSULA'S FISH AND CHIPS and featuring Ursula the sea witch in her glory days hung outside it. Painted wooden tentacles spiraled out of both sides of the building. The paint had faded, just like Ursula's powers, but the whites of Ursula's eyes still glowed in the gloom. Below the plaque was a sign that read YOU'LL TAKE IT HOW I MAKE IT! Below that was a lantern illuminating an inspection notice, marked "F" for *fail*, awarded by the Isle Department of Unhealth.

With his hook Harry lifted a string of silver fish from a pan resting on a dock beam, and he regarded a red-haired pirate holding a fishing rod. He tossed one of the fish back into the sea with a smile. The red-haired pirate looked on, mortified. Harry turned on his boot and sauntered through the seaweed-green swinging doors of the diner.

He entered the dumpy, smelly eatery, which was filled with slovenly scalawags hunched over mismatched tables. The place stank of rotten fish, which fit the filthy aesthetic: splintered dock beams, smashed lobster traps, an old waterlogged organ, chandeliers made out of steering wheels, and signs that said things like TIP OR ELSE! and EMPLOYEES MUST NOT WASH HANDS. Besides fish and chips, the diner sold other slop, such as sea slugs, gulf goo, and pickled lamprey. Harry stashed his sword in a rusty sword-check urn by the door that held others. Then he handed his string of fish to a diner and sashayed across the room.

He approached a long wooden table. Its stools were taken by a motley crew of dim-witted teen pirates who talked over trays of fish and chips. Among them was Gil, Gaston's brawny son, who had dirty blond hair peeping out from under a cap and wore an orange-brown leather vest. What Gil lacked in IQ he made up for in muscles. Harry knocked a pirate aside, used his stool to hop over the tabletop, and turned on the ancient fuzzy-screened TV by twisting a manual dial.

There was the infamous-on-the-Isle clip of Mal and Ben at their press conference.

A teenage girl with long turquoise hair plopped a tray of food down on the table in front of Harry, who looked hungrily at it. The girl wore a turquoise leather jacket with fringe epaulets, a fringe skirt, and a brown pirate's hat with starfish embroidered on it. She was every bit a pirate punk and also the spitting image of her sea witch mother, Ursula—back in the day, of course. Uma was the girl's name, and she wore Ursula's gold nautilus shell on a gold chain, though the necklace had no powers on the Isle of the Lost, where magic was forbidden and as obsolete as the old TV at which she glared.

Uma turned and grabbed fish sticks from Harry's tray, then chucked them angrily at the TV screen. "Ugh!" she yelled. She turned back to her pirate crew. "Poser," she shouted, referring, of course, to Mal.

"Traitor!" Harry called out at the TV.

Leaning on the table, Uma scanned the lounging pirates. *"Hello?"* she yelled.

The pirates instantly heaved every bit of food

within reach at the TV. They swore loudly, then slouched back into position and howled with wicked laughter.

Harry shook his fist at the TV. "I would *love* to wipe the smiles off of their faces! You know what I mean?" He grinned, and his scary-pretty eyes glinted.

Uma turned on dim-witted Gil, who was busy eating eggs. "Gil!" she barked.

"Huh?" asked Gil, completely and utterly unaware.

Uma leaned toward him. "You want to quit choking down yolks and get with the program?"

Gil mumbled with his mouth full of food and pointed. "Yeah, what they said!"

Uma turned back toward the others. "That little traitor, who left us in the *dirt*."

Harry sucked food off his fingers. "Who turned her back on evil," he said.

"Who said you weren't big or bad enough to be in her gang," Gil told Uma as he refilled his empty tray with food at a serving counter connected to the kitchen. "Back when you were kids. Come on, you guys remember," Gil said to a seething Uma. "She called her *Shrimpy*, and the name just kind of . . .

stuck." As he had been speaking, the pirates had all grown very quiet.

Uma rolled her eyes at Gil. "That snooty little witch, who grabbed *everything she wanted*," Uma snarled. "And left me nothing," she added quietly.

The pirates looked from Uma to each other solemnly.

"No," said Gil through a mouthful of soggy fries. "She left you that sandbox," he explained, oblivious to Uma's annoyance, "and then she said that you could have the shrimpy shovel—"

Uma wheeled on him. "I need you to stop talking."

"Look, *we* have her turf now," Harry told Uma. "They can stay in *Bore*-adon—"

"Harry, *that's* her turf now!" Uma cried, pointing at the TV showing Mal's press conference. She switched it off. "And I want it, too. We should not be getting her *leftovers!*"

She grabbed the arm of Harry's filthy red jacket. "Son of Hook!" she said. She latched on to Gil's bicep. "Son of Gaston!" She looked at the grimy ceiling. "And *me*, most of all, daughter of Ursula." She looked at Harry. "What's my name?" she asked.

Harry took off his hat and bowed down to her. "Uma," he said, smiling.

She stared at Gil, who looked up, startled. "What's my name?" she yelled.

"Uma?" he said through a mouthful of food.

She sighed and turned to the other pirates amassed before her at the table. "What's my name? What's my name?" she called out to them.

"Uma!" they boomed in unison.

That's right. Uma. She felt in her heart that she, not Mal, was the true Princess of Evil. Uma felt that she and her crew of pirates were the rottenest to the core. She'd show Mal . . . somehow. Uma strutted along the top of the long table, and her pirate crew cheered for her.

Just then, a long tentacle slithered out from the kitchen and lashed at Uma.

Shrieking, Uma leaped up and dodged it.

Her pirate crew ducked on the sides of the table to avoid it, too.

"Shut your clams!" bellowed Ursula's voice from the kitchen.

"Mooooom!" Uma shouted. She tossed back her

hair and regarded her pirates. "It's all right." Her voice got louder. "Because when I get *my* chance to rain down evil on Auradon, *I will take it*! They're gonna forget that girl. And remember the name—"

"*Shrimpy!*" yelled Gil, slamming his fists on the table.

Everyone looked at him in silence.

Harry glanced at Uma, who nodded. Harry then led Gil to the door and threw him out of the diner.

Uma was satisfied that Gil had gotten what he deserved. But she wouldn't truly be happy, not until Mal got what was coming to *her*.

CHAPTER NINE

BACK IN AURADON, THINGS AREN'T ALL THAT AND A BAG OF FISH AND CHIPS, EITHER. . . .

I'M RAMPING UP THE PRINCESS ACT FOR MY BIG DATE. HERE'S HOPING BEN BITES!

It was time for Mal and Ben's perfect picnic date at Reflection Pond.

Ben had brought Mal to a surprise picnic when she had first gotten to Auradon Prep. They had ridden through the countryside on his Vespa. Ben had then led her on foot through a grove. And after they had crossed an incredible suspension bridge with a beautiful stream below it, Ben had put a blindfold on Mal and led her gently down a dense forest path until eventually they stopped. When he had instructed her to open her eyes, they were at the Enchanted Lake, with its crystalline jade water and stone platform of ancient pillars wrapped in ivy and flowers. It was a surprise Mal would always cherish.

Today Mal was the one surprising Ben.

And she couldn't wait for the moment to end.

On a gazebo overlooking the calm green pond and surrounding lush tree-filled countryside, Mal and Ben sat at a table, covered by a gold tablecloth, which boasted all sorts of treats: soup, hors d'oeuvres, beef ragout, cheese soufflé, pies, puddings, pastel-colored cakes, fresh fruit tarts, a loaf of warm bread, and tiers of appetizers. All the fixings for a royal picnic to make Ben feel like a cherished guest.

"Would you like a hot hors d'oeuvre?" asked Mal. She wore a pale blue dress, and her long ice-blond hair was loose and down. She fed Ben with her hand.

Ben ate the appetizer, moaning. "This is the best thing I've ever had."

"So you like it?" asked Mal.

"I *more* than like it, in fact." Ben leaned in close to Mal and pinched a cracker from a tray, then sat back. "I double like it."

Mal giggled.

Ben gestured to a nearby bowl. "Beef ragout?" He picked up a bite with a fork.

"Did I surprise you? Did I do it?" asked Mal with a curious smile.

Ben took the big bite of the beef ragout. "Yeah. This is every single dish Mrs. Potts made for my parents! What did it take you—three days?" Ben surveyed the extravagant array of perfectly prepared fresh foods.

Mal eyed the picnic basket that sat on the table beside her. "Don't . . . even ask me," she said, laughing.

"Well, it means a lot that you stopped and did all this for me. With all the craziness that's been happening to you," said Ben. He took her hand in his.

Mal couldn't look Ben in the eyes. She stared down at the table and smiled.

Ben turned her face gently toward him. "I've missed you." He caressed her cheek. "We never have a lot of time to be just us."

It was true. Ben was busy being king and governing the United States of Auradon. And she was preoccupied with pretending to be his proper lady.

Mal wiped a drop of sauce from the corner of Ben's mouth.

Ben smiled. "Can't take me anywhere."

Mal laughed. She had said the same thing to him during their first picnic at the Enchanted Lake when she'd tried her first jelly doughnut and gotten sugar on her lips.

Mal was beginning to relax and enjoy herself.

Ben looked around. "Do you—do you have any napkins?" He reached for the picnic basket.

"I do, actually—" Mal said, feeling the moment slipping toward chaos. "I can grab them."

But before Mal could get his napkin, Ben reached into the picnic basket to look for one and instead pulled out Mal's spell book.

Mal gasped and froze.

Ben looked at the cover. "What's this?"

Mal stared at him, wide-eyed. "I . . . threw it in really last minute in case it rained and we needed to . . . I needed to step in." She attempted to take it from him.

Ben flipped through the various pages marked with sticky notes. " 'Speed-reading spell.' 'Blond hair spell . . . *Cooking* spell,'" Ben read. He looked at the picnic feast, slammed the book shut, and turned to Mal. "And here I was giving you props for fitting in so well! For doing your best!" Ben said loudly, shaking his head.

Mal began incanting a spell and waving her finger. *"Take back this moment that has passed. . . ."* She chewed her lip, trying to remember it. *"Replace it . . . Return it . . ."*

"Are you trying to *spell* me right now?"

"Ben, it has been *so* hard for me—"

"Mal!" Ben shouted. "Come on!" He stood and dropped the book onto the table. "Yeah, some things are hard! Do you think it's been easy learning how to be king?"

"No!" said Mal.

"I thought we were in this together!" Ben cried.

Mal bolted out of her seat. "We *are* in this together!"

"But we're not," Ben said. "We're not, Mal. You've been keeping secrets . . . and . . . and lying to me. I thought we were done with this. This isn't the Isle of the Lost, Mal!"

Mal was stung. "Believe me, I know," she said.

"Then why are you doing this?" Ben implored of her.

"Because I am *not* a pretty pink princess! I'm not one of those ladies, okay? I'm a big fake!" yelled Mal. She gestured to her hair and the food on the table. "I'm fake. This is fake." Sighing, she reached over the table, lifted her spell book, turned to a page, and incanted: *"Take this feast, this sumptuous meal, return it back to what is real."* She did a little finger wave and the feast disappeared. The trays, bowls, and plates of food were replaced by a sad peanut butter and jelly sandwich and a cookie.

"That's who I really am, Ben," said Mal, gesturing to the glum meal. Her eyes shimmered with tears, and she broke her stare with Ben to move away from him.

Ben reached out and touched her arm. "Mal," he said softly.

Mal shrugged Ben off. "No!" she said, and stomped away, leaving Ben alone.

Wanting to make her feel better, Ben picked up the sandwich and called out, "Peanut butter and jelly is my favorite!" But she was already gone. He walked back to the rail and gazed over the pond. Across the calm green water, Ben could see the land on the other side. He thought about how he'd spent many times looking out at the Isle of the Lost in the same far-off way.

Ben felt farther away from Mal than ever.

Once Mal got back to school, she burst into her dorm room and was relieved to find it empty.

Mal moved to Evie's worktable and found a small black box with a blue lid. She took a sharp pencil and stabbed the lid of the box repeatedly to make holes. "I don't belong here!" Mal cried out. She rushed to her mother's glass aquarium.

"Okay," Mal muttered, opening the top of the tank. She lifted the tiny lizard out of it and placed it into the black box. She looked down at her mother and let out a little laugh through her tears. "Let's blow this Popsicle stand, yeah?" asked Mal.

Auradon was not where she belonged—not anymore.

CHAPTER TEN

I KNEW TRYING TO BE BEN'S PERFECT GIRLFRIEND WAS A BAD IDEA.

I'M SO OUTTA HERE.

Mal rode her scooter out of the woods and came to a stop at the shore.

She looked across the Sea of Serenity at her far-off old home. The magical barrier flickered and shimmered over the Isle of the Lost like it was a memory, beckoning to Mal. She was still sobbing. She flipped her goggles onto her helmet and pulled her spell book out of her bag. She flipped through it and stopped. Then she incanted, *"Noble steed, proud and fair, you shall take me anywhere."* She waved her finger.

The scooter roared to life, bearing a new glittering graffiti paint job.

Mal put on her goggles and took a breath. "Please work." Her voice was desperate. She zoomed across the surface of the sea toward the isle of exiled prisoners, gaining speed. She headed toward the barrier, and her eyes grew wide.

With a flash, Mal's enchanted scooter disappeared through the barrier.

In no time, she rolled through a dusty lane filled with disheveled, grubby pirates selling knickknacks at their rotting storefronts. Her scooter was dinged and battered-looking, like it had taken a beating traveling through the barrier. A pirate leaped out of Mal's way. Another ducked behind the newspaper she had been reading. Mal stopped to scrutinize a vandalized Royal Cotillion poster of King Ben and the new blond version of herself in a pink dress with white lace gloves. It read THE EVENING'S EVENTS TO BE BROADCAST LIVE ON AURADON ROYAL TELEVISION. Over Ben's face, someone had scribbled a black eye patch and a goatee, and a purple X had been spray-painted over Mal's face with GOOD GIRL! on her body.

Mal thought back to a time when she had been

the vandal supplying the design, and she felt offended seeing that she'd become the vandal's victim, and strange that she was part of Ben's goodie reputation on the Isle. She wanted to shake that good-girl image—fast.

Mal flipped up her goggles. She ripped the poster down, crumpled it up, tossed it over her shoulder, snapped her goggles back down, and continued along her way. The destitute pirates looked on in her wake, frightened. Mal's scooter roared down another squalid street. People jumped out of the way. Some shook their fists at her.

Mal smiled. She was home.

A short distance later, Mal rolled through an alley infested with grungy thieves, minions, and pickpockets and parked her bike under the stairway of her crew's old hideout. It was a house perched high on a broken bridge's dilapidated support. There was a drop-down gate barring a flight of steps that led to the entrance at the top, where a sign read ISLE OF THE LOST in mismatched flickering letters. At the bottom of the hideout was an old-fashioned ship's call horn, where visitors could announce themselves. Mal removed her helmet, taking in her familiar surroundings.

She picked up a rock and hurled it at a sign that said DANGER: FLYING ROCKS, and the gate slid up. Mal ducked under it and climbed the steps. She paused on a landing to gaze over the Isle. It was as bleak and dismal as ever. She smirked and kept climbing until she reached the top, and she entered the vacant hideout. Exposed lightbulbs and bits of fabric clung to the ceiling, and graffiti images on the walls said WE SHALL RISE!, REVENGE!, and DOWN WITH AURADON!

The hideout was just how Mal and her friends had left it.

In Auradon, Ben reviewed official royal documents in his library office.

"Deborah, please ask Lumiere to call me regarding Cotillion. Thank you," he said into the earpiece he wore. He peered at the pile of papers stacked before him on the desk, framed on each side by the Auradon flag. He dipped his quill into an ink pot and took another paper with the Auradon crest at the top to review. The leather chair he sat in wasn't a throne, but it was the place where Ben performed most of his kingly duties when he wasn't in his official council meetings. The office was also somewhere to hide away when things got tough, like after the fight with Mal at the pond. Ben shook his head as if to make sense of it and signed the document. The framed portrait of him looked down on him from over the fireplace, as if it judged him.

Evie rapped on the door and stuck her face into the room. "Ben," she said softly.

Ben looked up, and his face brightened. "Evie! Come on in." He took out his earpiece.

She pushed through the door, closed it softly behind her, and faced Ben. Her lip trembled, and her eyes glistened. She held a piece of paper in her shaking hands. "Mal's gone back to the Isle," she said, "for good."

Ben's expression turned blank.

Evie walked to Ben's desk and handed the note to him. She also handed Ben's shiny gold beast-head ring to him. It had once belonged to his powerful father.

Ben's eyes widened. He took the note and read what Mal had written, then crumpled the paper in his hand. "This is my fault. This is my fault!" he roared. "I blew it. She's been under so much pressure lately. And instead of understanding, I—I just went all Beast on her!" Ben slumped over his desk. "I have to go there and apologize," he told Evie. "I have to go back! And beg her—"

"You'll *never* find her," said Evie.

Ben walked behind his desk to the window to look over the tree-filled lawn.

"You need to know the Isle, and how it works, and our hideouts. . . ." Evie exhaled. She looked thoughtful, then said, "You have to take me with you."

Ben spun away from the window. "Yes!" His face lit up. Then he squinted. "Uh, I mean, are you sure?"

Evie's expression hardened. "Yeah," she said, standing taller. "She's my best friend." Evie turned around. "And we'll take the boys, too, because there's safety in numbers. And none of us are all too popular over there right now."

"Thank you, Evie," said Ben.

Evie shifted to face him. "But first let's get two things straight," she said.

Ben stared at her, waiting.

"You have to promise me that I won't get stuck there again," said Evie.

"I promise," said Ben.

"Okay," she said.

Evie eyed Ben's royal-blue suit. "And there's no way you're going to the Isle looking like that."

CHAPTER ELEVEN

'VE BEEN ON THE ISLE FOR FIVE SECONDS AND I ALREADY FEEL *SO* MUCH BETTER.

NOW, TIME TO GET BACK IN TOUCH WITH MY VILLAIN ROOTS.

WHAT BETTER WAY THAN BY LOOKING LIKE MY BAD OLD SELF AGAIN?

Mal marched through narrow cobblestoned streets and reached Sorcerer's Square.

Around her, Isle ne'er-do-wells ambled to and fro below clotheslines heavy with damp, soiled garments, and merchants tinkered at their run-down ramshackle shop stalls with outdated objects and slop for sale. Mal made her way down the wet, slick street and approached the double doors of a shabby salon. A weathered sign above showed a giant pair of scissors and a perfume bottle bearing the words *Lady Tremaine's Curl Up and Dye.* Mal read a clock sign on one of the doors that said CLOSED UNTIL MIDNIGHT. She looked around, and when the coast was clear, she pushed open a door peeling with crusty paint and stole inside, quickly and quietly.

Mal stepped inside the decrepit building, pushed aside clear plastic panels, and found a girl sweeping a colorful salon. The place had pipes and wires exposed in the ceiling, hair dryers made with botched-together pieces of machinery, and steaming glass vials with colorful dyes percolating and running through a system of pipes over a bathtub. To top it all off, the entire place—from the walls, where cracked mirrors hung, to each janky mismatched salon chair—was splattered with streaks of every shade of bright neon dye.

Dizzy, Lady Tremaine's granddaughter, wore large gold-painted headphones embellished with tiny flowers and pearly metallic beads. Dizzy hadn't heard Mal come into the salon as she swept, moving as if she were ballroom dancing with the broom. She had on a multicolored dress and cat-eye glasses, and each of her nails was painted a different color. Her brown hair was back in a bun, and the ends were neon pink. Dizzy turned and saw Mal standing there, and she pulled off her headphones.

"Mal!" Dizzy's freckled face lit up. "Is Evie back, too?"

Mal let out a little laugh. "Ha. As if." She put her hand on her hip and looked around the salon. "I, uh, forgot that you guys don't open till midnight," she said.

Dizzy nodded.

"The place looks really good," said Mal.

Dizzy smiled. Even though she was only a few years younger than Mal, she looked up to her and valued her opinon.

Mal looked at Dizzy's gloves, her apron, and the pile of hair she had been sweeping. "So what is your deal? Has your grandmother given you any customers yet, or . . ."

Dizzy shrugged. "Just a witch here and there. Mostly it's a lot of scrubbing and scouring and sweeping." She looked at the pile of hair. "Lots and lots of sweeping . . ."

Mal snickered. "The old Cinderella treatment, hey?"

"Yeah. She's gone from wicked stepmother to wicked grandmother."

"That's not much of a leap. Hey, Dizzy, you used to do Evie, am I right?"

Dizzy beamed and nodded. "Yeah! I thought of the little braids!"

"Ya got any ideas for me?" asked Mal.

Dizzy sized Mal up and walked over to her. She picked up a strand of Mal's blond hair. "The washed-out blond with purple tips? The best of no worlds." She dropped the hair and examined Mal's face. "Hmmm, you cannot see where your face ends and your hair begins." She gestured to a nearby chair, which Mal quickly sat in. Dizzy snatched Mal's hand and peered at her fingernails. "Ugh! What is this? Bored to Death pink?" She spun Mal. "How far can I go?" she asked with a mischievous tone.

Mal smiled. "Honestly, the works," she said coolly. "I mean, whatever makes me feel like *me* but . . . way worse." She looked at Dizzy with her green eyes glinting.

"Yay!" Dizzy cheered and rushed to a table, where she lifted a pair of rusty garden shears. She opened and closed the blades twice, then spun back to Mal.

A grin spread across Mal's face. *Let the transformation begin!*

Dizzy got to work. First she dyed Mal's hair purple in the sink, used garden shears to trim Mal's purple locks, and pinned up soda cans in Mal's new do. Then Dizzy had Mal sit under a dryer so that her curls could set while Dizzy applied a fresh coat of wickedly black polish to Mal's nails. At last, Dizzy spun Mal around in her chair for the big reveal. Mal launched out of the chair and peered into the cracked fragments of the shattered mirror on the wall.

Mal's long lavender hair reached down past her shoulders, and her sparkling green eyes twinkled below new bluntly cut bangs. She beamed. Mal was the child of a villain through and through. Now it was undeniable.

Dizzy looked at her work, sporting the biggest smile imaginable.

"Ah! *There* I am," said Mal, delighted.

"Voilà!" squealed Dizzy.

"Voilà," said Mal, turning to Dizzy and holding out a couple of dollars to her.

Dizzy clutched her chest. "For *me*?" she asked incredulously.

Mal nodded. "Yeah! You earned it."

Dizzy took the money out of Mal's hand and marched across the salon to the cash register.

Harry Hook slipped through the front door and towered over the cash register. "Fork it over!"

Dizzy froze. Mal stood where she was, unnoticed by Harry.

Harry smirked at Dizzy with his hand outstretched.

Dizzy looked crestfallen. She slowly handed the cash to Harry.

"And the rest of it, *Four Eyes*," Harry sneered.

Dizzy moved around the cash register, opened it, and handed Harry everything that was inside. She leaned over the cashier desk and rested her chin glumly on her hand.

"Thank you." Harry turned to leave.

"Still running errands for Uma, or do you actually get to keep what you steal?" Mal piped up.

Harry whirled around and grinned when he saw her. "Well, well, well, isn't this a nice surprise?"

Mal smiled. "Hi, Harry."

Harry strolled toward her and waved his hook. "Wait until Uma hears that you're back. You know, she's never going to give you back your old territory."

Mal shook her head. "She won't have to." She nodded. "I will be taking it."

Harry flicked Mal's new do with his hook. "You know, I could hurt you."

Mal grabbed his wrist. "Oh, well . . ." She spit out the gum she had been chewing and stuck it on the tip of Harry's hook. "Not without her permission, I bet," she said, looking up at Harry.

Harry grinned, strode to the door, and stormed out, but not before he spun to knock knickknacks off the cash register counter and onto the floor with his hook.

Mal and Dizzy watched him leave.

Dizzy rolled her eyes. "Great," she said. "More sweeping."

~~~

Jay, Ben, Evie, and Carlos crept down a set of stairs toward the royal limo waiting outside. Thanks to Evie's sewing skills and talent for fashion design, Ben wore his new Isle-inspired outfit, which consisted of a distressed blue leather jacket with metallic studs, a blue beanie, blue fingerless leather gloves, blue pants, and dark boots. In fact, the whole gang was in their Isle of the Lost attire, with Evie stunning in a blue leather jacket and matching skirt; Jay in red-and-blue velvet pants, a leather jacket, and a beanie; and Carlos in red-and-black pants, a leather jacket, and fingerless gloves. They were ready for the Isle. It was not for the faint of heart. Their feet touched down on the pavement outside the school where the black stretch waited.

"Keys. Remote," said Ben, tossing them both to Jay. "Let's go."

"Wait!" said Evie.

Everyone gathered at the foot of the stairs.

"Something's wrong," she said.

Everyone looked at her expectantly.

She stepped in front of Ben, pulled his beanie

farther down over his hair, ruffled his jacket, and smiled. "There," she said, satisfied.

Suddenly, Dude appeared behind them on the stairs. "Road trip!" he said.

"Dude, no!" said Carlos. "Stay! The Isle is way too dangerous."

Ben, Evie, and Jay gawked at Dude.

"He just . . . talked?" asked Jay.

"Yeah. I know. I'll tell ya later," said Carlos.

Everyone stared at each other for a brief moment and shook their heads.

"Let's go," said Ben, determined to push through the shock of the talking dog.

In a haze, everyone climbed into the limo. Filled with buttons, gadgets, refreshments, and vast arrays of colorful sweets, it was the same one that had brought Mal, Evie, Jay, and Carlos to Auradon Prep. Jay and Carlos had tried their first-ever chocolate peanut butter cups in that very limo. But Jay had never driven it before. He smiled devilishly, grabbed the steering wheel, and hit the gas.

The limo rocketed away from the school.

CHAPTER TWELVE

Wicked new look? Check.
        Up next . . . taking my old turf back from Uma.

Night fell over the Isle of the Lost as the limo rolled to a stop in an empty warehouse.

Jay, Carlos, Evie, and Ben jumped out of the vehicle and slammed the doors. Around them were splintered wooden shipping crates, old sheets in a stinking pile, walls of corroded corrugated metal, and slimy barrels.

There was also a huge rusty metal pipe turned tunnel going into a rock wall.

"Ben," said Carlos, running to the pile of sheets. "Help me with the tarp."

Ben and Carlos carried the tarp to Evie and Jay,

and the four of them started to cover up the limo. After all, the car stood out like a shiny new penny in a garbage pile, and the friends didn't want to rouse any suspicious looks from possible passersby. That was the last thing they needed.

Evie looked around uneasily. "It's really weird being back," she told Jay.

"We'll get in and get out," he assured her.

"*Jay.*" Carlos got his attention and tossed half the tarp over the top of the limo to his friend.

Jay, along with Evie, took it, and they finished making sure the limo was completely hidden.

Meanwhile, Ben wandered to the giant rusty pipe tunnel. He peered inside it for a good long moment. "Hey! What's in here?" Ben called back to the others.

Carlos, Jay, and Evie rushed to Ben's side.

"You don't want to know," said Jay.

Carlos pulled Ben away from the opening.

"Hey, guys." Carlos turned to the whole group. "Keep it chill. All right? Last thing we need is our parents figuring out we're here."

His friends nodded in agreement as they all took off, away from the limo and around a dark bend.

They entered a seedy alleyway where tattered sheets hung from rickshaws and covered dirty entryways. Two unkempt children in shabby coats ran up to Evie, and one of them tried to pickpocket her.

"Hey," said Evie. "Hey! What are you doing?" She gripped an arm of each child.

They struggled against her, wriggling like eels.

"Stop!" said Evie. She released them, then reached into her pocket and held her tiny coin purse out to them. "Here. Just take it," she said, extending it to one.

The little kid grabbed it and scampered off.

Evie turned to Jay and Carlos, realizing Ben was nowhere in sight. "Ben," Evie said, sighing. The three marched down the alley to find him.

Ben had wandered ahead of his friends into a covered marketplace: Low Tide Lane, a remote alley where pirates sold their decrepit wares. He looked around at the clutter of barrels, lanterns, and splintered pieces of wood. Signs advertised crabgrass, grit, pond scum, and worms, and a black street sign with a double-sided white arrow pointing in opposite directions read NO WAY. Haggard pirates dozed behind their busted makeshift carts while others carried baskets of trash. Ben was in awe of the Isle, which until then had been a place he had only ever heard about.

It was far worse than he had expected. Yet he also found an odd beauty to it.

Ben's sights landed on a scrappy pirate, and Ben waved at him and smiled. The pirate glared back at him. Ben extended his arm and welcomed a hand-shake, but the pirate only lunged at Ben and growled.

Evie appeared with Jay and Carlos, and she gripped Ben's arm. "Stop it. Just stop."

Carlos stepped between Ben and the disgruntled pirate, ready to fight, but Jay yanked Carlos back. Now wasn't the time to be starting something. Luckily, the pirate wasn't interested in Carlos anyway.

Ben looked at his friends. *"What?"* he asked with a shrug, unsure of why they were so concerned. After all, he believed there was good in everyone—even there.

"This isn't a parade. This is the *Isle*," said Evie.

"Just keep your hands in your pockets unless you're stealing," said Jay.

"Yeah, you either slouch or you strut," said Carlos.

"And never, *ever* smile," said Evie.

Ben nodded. "Okay, thank you, guys—"

"No!" Evie motioned for silence. "Forget the thank-yous! And no *please*, either! Just . . . chill."

Evie, Carlos, and Jay went on to Ben about how he had to work on fitting in more on the Isle to throw off any suspicious looks. They explained the importance of dragging one's feet, nodding one's head, and leaning back. They preached to him not to care or stare and taught him how to watch his back, creep around, and chill like a true villain. Ben let it all sink in. Within moments, he began walking the walk and couldn't help smirking, pleased with himself for being able to fit in perfectly there. Not only did he look the part now, but he also acted it.

Now that Ben had mastered the art of appearing villainous, the crew headed through a sordid alley. It was finally time to find Mal and get her back.

Not far off, Gaston's oafish son Gil was pilfering eggs from a merchant. He had run out and needed more protein for his muscles. Gil turned and ran into Ben.

"Hey, man," Gil said angrily. He did a double take. "Hey, man . . . I know you!"

"Nope!" said Ben, shrugging and turning away. "I don't know you, either, so—"

"No, no, no! Yeah, you definitely know me! C'mon! C'mon, man, you know me. Okay, okay. I'll give you a hint, all right?" He grinned. "My dad is slick, quick, and his neck is incredibly thick."

Ben looked at him blankly, then exchanged glances with his friends.

"Nothing?" asked Gil. "Come on, man. You're—" Gil, in his fingerless yellow gloves, pointed at a poster of King Ben on the alley wall that had RIDE WITH THE TIDE spray-painted over it in black paint. Then Gil pointed to Ben. Then he did that a few more times until it all began to sink in. He was a little slow, to say the least. "Whoa, you're King Ben!" Gil exclaimed.

"Uh, let's go," said Evie, guiding Ben past Gil, with Jay and Carlos flanking them.

"Yeah, no, you totally are King Ben!" cried Gil, watching as they passed. "And you're Jay, Carlos, Evie—hey, guys!" he said cheerily. Then his expression set into a huge oafish grin. "Uma's gonna love this!" He could barely contain his excitement. Gil turned and hurried off.

Before long, Jay, Evie, Ben, and Carlos arrived at the foot of the bridge hideout, where they knew they would find Mal. Ben noticed her scooter lying on its side under the stairs, and he inspected its beat-up, graffitied varnish. He had never imagined his gift would take her to the Isle.

Meanwhile, Jay grabbed a rock and lobbed it at the sign. The gate glided up, and Jay steered Ben toward the stairs. Ben peered into the darkness of the staircase that wound its way to the top of the hideout; then he looked back at his friends.

"Wish me luck." Ben started up the stairs.

Watching him vanish, Jay, Evie, and Carlos leaned and sat, prepared to wait.

ALTHOUGH MAL WAS LIVING THE LIFE OF A PRINCESS IN AURADON, SHE COULDN'T HELP FANTASIZING ABOUT ALL THE WAYS TO BE WICKED.

LONNIE CHALLENGED THE RULE THAT SAID SHE COULDN'T JOIN THE R.O.A.R. TEAM BECAUSE SHE WAS A GIRL. EVEN CHAD KNEW SHE COULD OUT-SPAR HIM.

WHEN MAL GOT TO THE ISLE, SHE LEARNED THERE WAS A NEW BAD GIRL RULING HER OLD STOMPING GROUND. WHAT'S HER NAME? UMA, DAUGHTER OF URSULA.

BEN WANTED TO FIND MAL AND BRING HER BACK TO AURADON. BUT FIRST HIS FRIENDS HAD TO SHOW HIM THE ART OF CHILLIN' LIKE A VILLAIN.

IN THE HIDEOUT, MAL TOLD BEN THAT SHE WASN'T GOING BACK TO AURADON WITH HIM.

CARLOS AND JAY WERE WORRIED. UMA HAD CAPTURED BEN, AND MAL INSISTED ON HANDLING THE SITUATION BY HERSELF.

STRENGTH RULES: IF MAL WON THE ARM WRESTLING MATCH WITH UMA, THEN KING BEN WOULD BE FREE TO GO.

DIZZY, DAUGHTER OF DRIZELLA, WAS LIKE A LITTLE SISTER TO EVIE. PLUS, THEY SHARED A PASSION FOR FASHION.

MAL PROMISED EVIE THAT NO MATTER WHERE THEY WERE, THEY'D ALWAYS BE BEST FRIENDS.

HARRY HOOK, SON OF CAPTAIN HOOK, COUNTED DOWN THE MINUTES TILL HE COULD MAKE BEN WALK THE PLANK.

IT WAS FAIRY GODMOTHER'S MAGIC WAND IN EXCHANGE FOR KING BEN'S LIFE. HOPEFULLY UMA WOULDN'T BE ABLE TO SPOT THE WAND WAS A FAKE.

HARRY CACKLED AS UMA TOLD MAL THAT TIME WAS RUNNING OUT.

MAL AND UMA SWUNG THEIR SWORDS IN A VICIOUS MATCH. TALK ABOUT CUTTHROAT COMPETITION!

THANKS TO DUDE'S ADVICE, CARLOS HAD FINALLY GOTTEN THE COURAGE TO TELL JANE HOW HE FELT ABOUT HER.

FLASH! SNAP! THE PAPARAZZI SWARMED EVIE WITH QUESTIONS ABOUT THE GOWNS SHE HAD DESIGNED FOR COTILLION. AND DOUG COULDN'T HAVE BEEN MORE PROUD.

CHAPTER THIRTEEN

MY OLD HIDEOUT DEFINITELY AIN'T WHAT IT USED TO BE.
NOTHING A LI'L SPRAY PAINT CAN'T FIX, THOUGH.

Inside a shoddy tower, Ben climbed the steps toward
the sound of hissing spray paint.

He stopped on a platform, noticing the grimy,
dank vibe, and then followed the noise down a flight
of steps into Mal's hideout. Eyes wide, he took in the
graffitied walls and continued to make his way farther into the room.

He stopped short. There was Mal. She stood on
an old trunk facing the wall and worked furiously
on a self-portrait of a wild purple-haired Isle version
of her tearing her way out of the ice-blond Auradon
princess version of her.

Talk about making a statement.

Ben quietly approached Mal. "At least I don't see a picture of me with horns and a pitchfork," he said jokingly.

Mal whipped around. "Ben," she said, surprised.

He took another step toward her.

She held out her hand, motioning for him to stop.

Ben froze. "Mal, I'm so sorry about our fight. It was all my fault." He held out his beast-head ring. "Please come home."

Mal stepped down off the trunk, hanging her head, and tossed the spray paint can into a rusty shopping cart with a clatter. "Ben, *this* is my home," said Mal softly. She stopped in front of Ben, leaving some space between them.

Ben smiled warmly at her. "I brought the limo. It's a sweet ride."

Mal looked at his beast-head ring for a moment, then folded her arms. "I don't fit in. I really tried, Ben. I *really* gave it a shot. And if you think I can change, I think you're *wrong*."

Ben opened his arms. "Then *I'll* change. I'll skip

school, I'll blow off some of my responsibilities—"

"No! No!" Mal shook her head. "See? I am such a terrible influence! I mean, it's only a matter of time before I do something so messed up that the people turn on not only me, but they turn on *you*!"

Ben took Mal's hand. "Don't quit *us*, Mal. The people love you. *I* love you." He handed her the ring.

Mal stared at Ben in silence. She wasn't quite sure what to say.

"Don't *you* love *me*?" Ben asked quietly.

Mal took his beast-head ring, put it in his hand, and closed it. "I have to take myself out of the picture, because it's what's best for you and it's what's best for Auradon."

Ben took a step toward her. "Mal, please."

Mal put her hand on his chest to stop him. "I can't do this." She turned and walked back to the shopping cart, where she picked up the spray paint can. "You have to go," she said. She stepped up on the trunk and faced the wall. Then she turned and saw that Ben was still standing there. "Ben, please go. Please leave."

Ben hung his head and slowly backed out of the room until he was out of sight.

Suddenly, Mal felt as shaken as her spray paint can. She tried her hardest not to cry.

Outside, Carlos, Jay, and Evie stirred as they heard Ben heading down the stairs.

The gate slid up, Ben walked out, and then the gate started closing behind him. "She's not coming back," he said, walking past them and down the abandoned alley.

Evie's mouth was agape. "What?" she exclaimed.

Carlos and Jay exchanged alarmed looks.

Evie walked to the gate, but it slammed shut. She was too late. She walked to the call horn and spoke into it. "M? Mal? Just let us up. We just want to talk."

Inside the hideout, Mal had pulled a giant lever to lock the gate. Her voice sounded through the horn. *"Go away!"*

Evie, Jay, and Carlos looked at each other, at a loss.

Jay rested a hand on Evie's shoulder. "Let's just

give her a couple of hours to cool off, all right?"

Carlos looked down the alley, which fluttered with rags. "Guys . . ." he said.

Jay and Evie gathered beside him, and Evie said, "What?"

"Where's Ben?" asked Carlos.

Evie peered down the dim alley. "Ben?" she called out.

A dark silhouette walked toward them.

"Ben?" Evie sighed, relieved. "Ben! Don't scare us like that."

The figure stepped closer. But it wasn't Ben.

"Don't scare you?" Harry repeated sweetly. "You see, but that's my specialty."

"Harry," gasped Evie.

Jay took a step toward him. "What did you do with Ben?" he demanded.

"Hmmm? Oh! We nicked him. Yeah, and if you ever want to see him again, have Mal come to the chip shop tonight. Alone. Uma wants a little visit." Harry smiled and looked at them, landing his sights on Jay. "Aww. Seems you've lost your edge, Jay."

Jay lunged at him, but Carlos held Jay back.

Harry giggled, then began to whistle as he strolled off down the alley.

Evie, Jay, and Carlos looked on, horrified.

Inside the hideout, Mal confronted Evie, Jay, and Carlos. "If you guys never would have brought him here, this never would have happened! What were you thinking?" Mal yelled.

"M, he was going to come with or without us. We wanted to protect him," said Evie.

"Yeah, which we *blew*," added Carlos, throwing his arms up.

"Okay, okay. So what are we gonna do?" asked Jay.

"*We* are not doing anything," Mal insisted, stopping in front of her friends. "This is between Uma and me. She's a punk, and now *I* need to go get him." She picked up her leather-studded backpack from the dusty old couch.

She could feel the weight of her spell book inside it. *Wish I could use it here to get us out of this,* she thought. *Dumb Auradon rules strike again.*

"Whoaaa, Mal. You're gonna have to go through Harry Hook and his wharf rats, and Gil . . ." said Carlos.

"Exactly. You need us," said Jay.

Mal shook her head. "Uma said to come alone."

Evie put her hands on her hips. "Mal, come on."

Carlos shrugged and looked at Evie and Jay. "She doesn't have a choice."

Evie sighed, knowing he was right.

"I know one thing," said Carlos. "I'm not going anywhere." He sat on the couch.

Jay nodded. "We'll be here when you get back."

CHAPTER FOURTEEN

U GH! SERIOUSLY, WHY DID MY FRIENDS HAVE TO COME HERE? ONCE I GET BEN BACK FROM UMA, I'LL SEND EVERYONE ON THEIR WAY. P.S. I CAN'T WAIT TO SEE THE LOOK ON UMA'S FACE WHEN I TELL HER THAT THE PRINCESS OF EVIL IS BACK AND HERE TO STAY.

In her apron, Uma emerged from the kitchen in Ursula's Fish and Chips.

She carried a tray of fish and chips in each hand and dropped one onto the long wooden table in front of an old pirate who looked like she wore a potato sack. The fish and chips flew off the tray with the impact and landed on the dirty table.

"Hey! I wanted the fried clams!" the angry customer shouted at Uma.

The other diners looked up from their tables at the outburst.

Uma wheeled menacingly on the customer. "And I wanted a sea pony. Life ain't fair."

The customer recoiled.

Uma strolled across the diner and roughly slid the other tray of food onto a table. "Order up," she mumbled. She looked up, and a smile spread across her face as she watched the dingy green doors to the diner open and Mal strut into the building.

Mal paused in the doorway. "I'm baaa-ack!" she sang.

Uma cackled. "Loser, party of one," she said. "Right this way, please." She gestured toward an empty table. As Mal approached it, Uma kicked a chair toward her. But Mal was quick and caught it by its back, turned it around, and plopped down into it in front of the table. Uma crossed her arms, watching.

Mal smiled smugly. "Place still stinks," she noted.

"Oh, I'm sorry," said Uma with feigned concern. "We're down a butler today, *princess*." She cackled again and looked around the fetid diner at her fellow pirates.

"Where is he?" asked Mal, getting down to business.

Uma plucked off her soiled apron, dropped it onto the floor, and started to pace in front of Mal. "You know, I've dreamed of this," said Uma with a smile. Then her expression hardened. "*You* needing something from *me*, and me watching you squirm like a worm on a hook." Uma looked at the pirates, who nodded. Uma smiled again.

Mal let out a short laugh. "I'm so flattered that you dream of me. I haven't given you a single thought since I left."

"Oh, obviously," said Uma, stooping so that her face was inches from Mal's. "You have your perfect little life, don't you? And we're twenty years into a garbage strike." Uma walked around the table and put a hand on the chair across from Mal.

"Listen, if you have some kind of score to settle with me, game on! I see no need to bring Ben into this," said Mal.

"Oh, it may not be necessary, but it is *so* much fun." Uma walked back around the table and moved her face close to Mal's again. She smiled. "Here's the deal," she said.

Mal interrupted her with a laugh. "Just like your mother. Always a catch."

Uma rolled up her sleeves and sat across from Mal. She slammed her elbow onto the table as if she was about to arm wrestle. "If you win, Ben is free to go," she said.

Mal liked a challenge. She rested her elbow on the table.

The diners noticed something was going on and got up from their tables to crowd around them.

Uma grinned. "Oh, don't you want to know what I get if *I* win?"

"Still dreaming," said Mal.

Uma chuckled. "You know, as I recall, your mother thought she had things all sewn up, too," said Uma. "How'd that work out for her?"

Good one, thought Mal. "On three," she said, locking eyes with Uma.

"One," said Uma with a smile.

"Two," Mal said flatly, betraying zero emotion.

"Three," they said in unison.

Mal and Uma started to arm wrestle, not taking their eyes off each other. Their arms quivered. The pirates looked on, whispering among themselves.

"You know, that whole princess act?" said Uma. "I never bought it for a second. You can stick a tiara on a villain, but you're still a villain, honey."

"Aw, and you can throw a pirate hat on, but you're still Shrimpy," said Mal.

Uma faltered for a split second but then regained control. Mal's eyes flashed green. She pushed Uma's hand down so that it was mere inches from the table.

"If *I* win," said Uma through bared teeth, "you bring me the wand."

Mal gawked, and the green light drained from her eyes. In that moment, Uma rammed Mal's arm down onto the table. Mal gasped. Uma howled with laughter. The pirates around them cheered, and Uma stood and threw her hands up victoriously.

Uma hunched over the table and glowered at

Mal. "Now, if you want beasty boy back, bring Fairy Godmother's magic wand to my ship tomorrow at twelve o'clock noon. *Sharp!*" Uma started to walk away. "Oh, and if you blab, you can kiss your baby good-bye." Uma sauntered off and left Mal shaking her head.

Losing to Uma had *not* been part of Mal's plan.

CHAPTER FIFTEEN

GREAT. WE STILL DON'T HAVE BEN SAFE AND SOUND. AND NOW I HAVE TO GET MY HANDS ON THE WAND. WOULDN'T BE THE FIRST TIME. ONLY, THIS TIME IT'S A MATTER OF LIFE OR DEATH.

NO PRESSURE, MAL.

Inside the bridge hideout, Mal relayed the dire news to her friends.

Carlos was seated at the desk, Jay was sprawled out on the couch, and Evie stood behind him. They watched Mal pace back and forth.

"Ugh! There's *no* way we're going to give Uma the wand," said Evie. "Are you kidding, like we're just going to let her *destroy* Auradon?" She threw her hands up.

"We don't give Uma the wand and Ben is toast, guys," said Carlos.

"Yeah, what other option do we have?" asked Jay.

"So we give Fairy Godmother's wand to *Uma*, of all people—" started Evie.

Mal held out her hands. "You guys!" she said.

They quieted down and gave her their attention.

Mal gestured to Carlos. "Your 3-D printer. Is there any way that you could—"

"A phony wand," said Carlos with a snap of his fingers. "In my sleep!"

"The second Uma tests it, she'll know it's fake," Evie rebutted.

"Okay," said Mal. "So then we just get Ben out really fast. We need some kind of diversion!"

"Smoke bombs!" shouted Jay.

Mal pointed at him and nodded.

"Perfect!" said Evie, walking over to Mal. "I can get the chemicals I need at Lady Tremaine's place." She stopped in front of Mal. "Oh, and *sick* hair, by the way," she said, lightly touching it. "Wicked stepmom's *seriously* stepped up her game!"

"Do you want to know something? *Dizzy* did this!" said Mal.

Evie smiled. "*Little Dizzy?* Shut up!"

Carlos rested his face in his hand while Jay walked over to join him.

"I know, and I'm, like, seriously loving it!" Mal ran her fingers through her hair.

"I'm, like, really proud of her!" Evie said.

"Right?" said Mal.

Jay nudged Carlos and cleared his throat.

"Uhhh, *helloooo!*" Carlos called out.

Mal and Evie turned to him and Jay.

"Right," Evie said quietly, realizing they should get back on track.

Mal clapped. "Okay. Jay. Carlos. You meet us at Pirate's Cove no later than noon. And, guys, *losing* . . . Hey!" Mal snapped her fingers to get their full attention. "It's not an option." She looked gravely from Evie to Jay to Carlos. "Because we're rotten . . ."

"To the core," the friends said in unison.

CHAPTER SIXTEEN

T FEELS GOOD PLOTTING AND PLANNING WITH MY FRIENDS. JUST LIKE OLD TIMES. I'VE SERIOUSLY MISSED THAT.

Mal and Evie entered Lady Tremaine's Curl Up and Dye and crept up behind Dizzy.

She was hunched over her table, which was piled with knickknacks, making a colorful headband. Evie snuck up beside her and tapped her shoulder to get Dizzy's attention.

Dizzy beamed, jumped up, and hugged Evie. "Evie? Evie! You came back!"

"Oh, my Dizzy," said Evie, taking the younger girl's hands in her own.

Mal looked on and chuckled. "It's so great to see you, too," she said drily.

"Is it all just like we imagined?" Dizzy asked Evie,

wanting to know all about Auradon. "Do they really have closets you can walk into?"

Evie giggled at her earnest questions.

"Have you been in real a swimming pool? What does ice cream taste like?" asked Dizzy.

Evie laughed. "It's cold and sweet, and if you eat it too fast, it gives you a headache," she said, stooping low so that she and Dizzy were eye to eye.

"Really?" Dizzy squealed.

Evie nodded.

"I saved your sketchbook for you!" said Dizzy, bolting across the salon.

"You did?" Evie asked Dizzy, looking at Mal. Evie put a hand to her heart.

Dizzy raced back to them, carrying a thick blue book that had a red heart topped with a gold crown on its intricately decorated cover.

"Dizzy!" cried Evie. She sat down in front of the book at the table and beamed.

Mal stroked Evie's hair affectionately, and Dizzy smiled over her shoulder.

"Oh, my gosh," said Evie as she opened the beautiful book to a drawing of a short yellow-and-blue dress. There was some lacy blue fabric pinned to the page. "I made this dress out of an old curtain and safety pins," she said, relishing the memory.

"Yeah! It reminds me of the dress you made for Mal when she met Jasmine," said Dizzy.

"I spilled curry all over it," said Mal.

Evie and Dizzy laughed.

"Yeah, I saw that," said Dizzy.

Mal left them to inspect another table that boasted an assortment of items. After all, they were at the salon for a reason. They needed smoke bomb supplies.

Meanwhile, Evie tapped the dress design with her fingertips. "You're totally right, Dizzy," she said. "This was totally the inspiration for that."

"I knew it!" Dizzy punched a gloved fist up into the air. "You can take the girl out of the Isle, but you can't take the Isle out of the girl!" She pressed her cheek to Evie's.

Behind them, Mal picked up a plastic bowl and began to fill it with shower caps. She had an idea, and she was going with it. *This just might work,* she thought.

Evie closed her sketchbook, and she picked up a

shiny metallic accessory and a tiny gold crown. She held the crown against the accessory, creating a hair ornament. "Is this too much?" she asked Dizzy. "Or is this fabulous?"

Dizzy struck a pose and extended her arm. "Hand me the glue gun!"

Back at Auradon Prep, Jay and Carlos walked down the hallway to their dorm room. Dude bounded toward them, obviously excited that they were finally back.

"Sorry I'm so late," Carlos whispered to Dude. "Ben got taken."

"Why's our door open?" asked Jay.

He and Carlos entered the room and found Chad printing on the 3-D printer.

"Are you *kidding* me?" yelled Carlos.

Chad jumped and looked up. "I knocked," he explained.

Carlos held out his hand and looked at Chad until Chad gave him the copy of his room key. Then Carlos canceled Chad's print job, pulled the object from the tray, and handed it to Jay.

"What *is* it?" Jay asked Chad.

"A Chad action figure," said Chad. "Minus the head," he added.

"Sounds like an improvement," mumbled Carlos. He moved around the printer and quickly programmed it to make the sparkling silver wand from a photo on his phone.

As the wand began to appear, Chad peered at it curiously. "Why are you making Fairy Godmother's wand?" he asked.

Carlos looked at Jay. "Umm . . . why *are* we making the wand?"

"Ben's been captured!" said Dude.

"*What?*" shouted Chad. He did a double take. "Dude can talk?"

Carlos looked at Dude. "I was stalling," Carlos said from the side of his mouth.

Dude wagged his tail. "I thought you forgot," he said.

"You can't tell *anyone*," Jay said to Chad. "Ben's life depends on it."

Little did they know that outside their dorm room, Lonnie, who had dropped by to ask Jane about her Cotillion dress, had heard the whole thing. She gasped and sprinted down the hall.

Chad furrowed his brow. "If something were to happen to him . . ." He smiled at the boys. "You know . . . what I'm saying. . . ." He waggled his eyebrows.

"Something bad, I get it," said Carlos, rolling his eyes.

"God forbid," said Chad, feigning concern. "Who do you think might be next in line to be king?"

Jay looked at Carlos. "Is it me, or is that in really poor taste?"

As Chad left their room, Jay made sure to slam the door behind him. Carlos quickly punched some numbers into the printer, and the machine whirred to life.

CHAPTER SEVENTEEN

EVIE IS A WIZARD AT CHEMISTRY.
THESE SMOKE BOMBS ARE ALMOST DONE!
KIDS, DON'T TRY THIS AT HOME.

Night fell on the Isle, and Mal and Evie had transformed the salon into a laboratory.

They wore plastic gloves and stood beside the dye-streaked bathtub and percolating glass vials. Evie mixed vibrant powders as Mal funneled them into the shower caps, which she tied off. Dizzy sat at her table, crafting her fashion accessory.

Evie picked up Dizzy's headband and held it over her head. "M, how amazing would this look with my shredded tee and heart purse?"

"Very amazing," said Mal sincerely.

"Right?" asked Evie.

"Yeah," said Mal.

"Take it," Dizzy told Evie, standing. "Take a bunch!"

"Dizzy!" squealed Evie, overjoyed at her generosity.

Dizzy grabbed a handful of barrettes, headbands, and wraps from her table and raced to Evie, who held open her red purse.

"Thank you," said Evie.

"It would make me so happy to know you were wearing something of mine in Auradon," said Dizzy. "Almost like me being there myself."

Evie pulled Dizzy in for a hug and sighed. "I wish I could take you with me."

"At least one of us had her dream come true, right?" said Dizzy with a smile.

Mal dropped the last of the shower-cap smoke bombs into her backpack, right alongside her trusty old spell book. "E, we gotta go."

Evie and Dizzy looked at each other again; then Dizzy bowed and skipped back to her table. Evie could barely take her eyes off Dizzy. Evie and Mal headed to the door with Mal's backpack full of smoke bombs and then turned back to look at Dizzy.

They watched Dizzy open Evie's sketchbook and lovingly flip through it.

"She'll be okay," Mal assured Evie.

Evie nodded. "Yeah," she said quietly. "But she could be so much more."

"Let's go," said Mal, reaching out.

"Okay," said Evie, taking Mal's hand.

They ducked through the plastic panels and out the front doors of the salon.

Mal and Evie made their way through the decrepit alleys of their childhood.

Her arm linked with Mal's, Evie smiled at her friend as they walked down a dark lane. "Do you remember coming here while our moms fought over the best way to poison a princess?"

"Yeah! Apple or spindle? That one was epic. That went on for actual days." Mal chuckled.

"Like it mattered, right?" said Evie. "They were both undone by True Love's Kiss."

"Works every time," said Evie and Mal in unison, breaking into laughter.

They slowed in front of the entrance to the bridge hideout.

"I really thought that's what you and Ben had," Evie said. She looked at Mal. "Do you want to talk about it?"

Mal's smile vanished as quickly as it had arrived. "I'm not coming back, Evie."

Evie looked long and hard at Mal and unhooked her arm to face her.

"I can't," said Mal. "I really tried to tell you."

Evie sighed and leaned against a support beam.

"I . . . just . . . I don't know," said Mal. "I saw your face and how it lit up and how incredibly happy you were that first day that we went into our rooms, and I couldn't—I could *not* spoil that for you." Mal remembered when she and Evie had first entered their dorm room at Auradon Prep. At the sight of the room, dappled in sunlight, with the flowery curtains fluttering gently in the fresh breeze, Evie had squealed with delight as she took in their new home. But Evie had tried to hide her excitement to match Mal's disgust, and the two of them together had closed the frilly pink curtains and plunged the dorm into darkness. Mal knew that if Evie and she were to follow their hearts, what Evie wanted was light, while what Mal wanted was . . .

Evie sighed. "Well, if you're staying here, then I'm staying with you."

"No," said Mal, wincing. "Evie—you are an Auradon girl. And I am, and will always be, the girl from the Isle." Mal picked up a rock, chucked it at the sign, and gestured for Evie to follow her up into the hideout. They ducked under the gate.

Evie and Mal climbed the flights of steps. Evie stopped on a landing and looked out over the Isle. Mal stood beside her at the railing. They looked at each other, taking a moment to accept that in the end, they belonged in different worlds. Each girl knew in her heart that they'd always still be with each other in spirit when the day finally came for them to part ways. They'd know then that they'd meet again.

Even if it was in the space between.

~~~

Carlos and Jay had fallen asleep waiting for the 3-D printer to produce the wand.

They sat side by side in chairs, and Carlos's head rested on Jay's. Jay lifted his head, smacked Carlos, calling out his name, and stood up from his chair.

"Huh? What?" Carlos jerked awake, saw the wand, and bolted up.

It looked exactly like Fairy Godmother's wand. It sparkled as if it were full of all the power of the real thing.

Carlos lifted it up. "Not bad," he said.

"Yeah," Jay said with a nod. He took the fake wand and turned to Carlos.

"Let's go," they said in unison, moving to the door.

Dude bolted up from his doggy bed on Carlos's bed.

Carlos turned to him. "No, Dude. You stay," he said. "I'm serious. *Stay.* I love you, buddy. We'll be back before you know it!" He followed Jay out of the dorm.

They ran down the hall and exited into the night.

As soon as they cleared the front steps of the building, they bumped into Doug.

Jay hid the replica wand behind his back.

"Hey! Have you seen Evie?" Doug asked them.

Jay and Carlos exchanged a long look.

"She . . . went camping," lied Carlos.

Jay nodded.

"Evie 'I Want to Live in a Castle'? Sleeping on the ground with no place to plug in a hair dryer?" Doug narrowed his eyes at Carlos, then analyzed Jay's poker face.

Jay and Carlos burst into laughter, shrugging.

"You know how spontaneous she is," Carlos told Doug, making light of Doug's concern. He laughed again, and he and Jay backed away from Doug. They had taken only a few steps when Lonnie stepped out from behind a stone column. She wore her R.O.A.R. uniform and carried a quiver of swords over her shoulder.

"I'm coming with you guys," she said confidently.

"*What?* We don't need to have swords at the . . . Waffle Hut," Jay fibbed.

Lonnie raised her eyebrows. "You guys are going to the Isle to rescue Ben, and it's either you take me or . . . I'm going to have to tell Fairy Godmother."

Jay and Carlos glanced at each other and then gulped. After realizing they had no choice, they slowly nodded.

Lonnie giggled and threw an arm around each of their necks, beaming her hundred-watt grin. "This is going to be great!" she said as the trio went on their way.

If only Lonnie knew what they were in for . . .

CHAPTER EIGHTEEN

WHAT IS IT ABOUT THE CLOCK STRIKING TWELVE AND MAGIC WANDS?

WE NEED TO HURRY AND SAVE BEN—BEFORE WE *ALL* WALK THE PLANK!

It seemed to be just another bleak windy day at Pirate's Cove.

The wharf bustled with patchy pirates, sullied scalawags, and mumbling merchants. Nothing seemed to be out of the ordinary. But despite appearances, that day was different. For at the bottom of the decaying multilevel pier, there was a captive inside the old pirate ship with dark octopus insignia on the sails and young pirates patrolling the deck. It was none other than Ben, who had been tied with rope to the mainmast.

Harry leaped onto the main deck and landed in front of Ben. He put his face close to Ben's. "Coochy coochy coooo," he teased, grazing Ben's chin with the curve of his sharp hook. Harry laughed. "How's it feel to be king now, eh?"

Uma strolled up and pushed Harry away from Ben. "Ugh, give it a rest, Harry. We don't want damaged goods." She sat on a trunk in front of Ben and watched him.

"*You* said I could hook him," Harry snarled at Uma. He hung by an arm from salt-encrusted rigging ropes like a monkey, pointing his hook menacingly at Ben's neck.

"I said at *noon*," Uma corrected him.

Harry jumped down and stepped beside Ben, pressing his face close to Ben's again and dangling Captain Hook's silver clock by his cheek. "Twenty minutes to go," he said.

"It says eleven-thirty," said Ben.

Harry leered at Ben with his light eyes bulging.

"You better hope your girlfriend comes through," said Uma.

"She's not my girlfriend anymore," Ben added.

"Hmmm." Uma turned to Harry. "Harry, leave us alone."

Harry checked his father's clock and walked up to Ben. "Nineteen minutes to go," he said. He slid the watch over Ben's shoulder threateningly, then twirled it on its silver chain as he backed away, leaving Ben and Uma alone.

"I get that you don't deserve this—" Ben started.

Uma cackled. "*This?* This island is a prison, thanks to *your father!*" shouted Uma. "And don't pretend to look out for me, because no one's looking out for me. It's just me."

"This isn't your mother's plan?" asked Ben. "Isn't that her necklace?" He nodded, indicating the gold shell hanging from Uma's neck on a chain.

Uma let out a laugh and shook her head. "She doesn't care about me, either. Well, not unless she needs someone for the night shift."

"Ouch," said Ben.

"I don't need your pity!" yelled Uma.

"No, you certainly don't. You're very resourceful. I don't see *you* tied up."

Uma stood up and stepped in front of Ben. She crossed her arms. "So, let's trash-talk Mal," she said with a devilish grin.

"I'd rather talk about you," Ben said kindly.

Uma laughed. "Oh, funny *and* a gentleman. I really hope I don't have to feed you to the fishes."

"You don't," said Ben. "Set me free and we'll go back together."

"Oh, so *now* I get an invite?" Uma howled. "Gee, I wonder why." She brought her face inches from Ben's. "You know, when you brought Mal, Evie, Carlos, and Jay to Auradon . . . that's as mad as I've ever been in my life. And *believe me*, I've been plenty mad." She tapped Ben's cheek a few times and turned away from him. She folded her arms across her chest once again.

"I never thought that I could have hurt the people that weren't picked," said Ben, looking at the back of Uma's pirate hat.

She whipped around and unfolded her arms. She was all ears.

"My plan was to start with four kids and then bring more people over, but I—but I guess I was busy being king," said Ben as he looked at Uma. "That sounds lame. I'm so sorry."

Uma nodded, and her expression softened.

"You're a leader, Uma. So am I. Come to Auradon and be part of the solution."

Uma looked Ben dead in the eye. "*Me*. Part of your solution," she said.

Ben looked at her for a long hopeful moment.

She shook her head. "Hmmm. Nah, I don't need *you*." She jabbed a finger at Ben's chest. "I'm gonna get there on my own." She looked at the pirates and barked, "Harry!"

He marched over to them.

Uma touched her shell necklace. "And see what this puppy can do," she added.

Mal and Evie waited in the noxious alley outside the rusty pipe tunnel.

The royal limo rolled up in front of them, and Jay, Lonnie, and Carlos got out.

"I'll grab the swords," Jay told Lonnie.

"Okay," said Lonnie, closing the door.

Jay raced to the trunk.

Lonnie approached Mal and Evie.

"Lonnie!" exclaimed Mal.

Lonnie smiled. "I made them bring me."

"Oh! I'm so glad," said Mal.

Lonnie hugged Mal, then Evie.

"Welcome to the Isle," said Evie. "It's good to see you."

"Thanks," Lonnie replied.

"We brought swords," Jay told Carlos. He opened the trunk of the limo and pulled out the quiver of swords, revealing Dude, who peeked up from a blanket.

"And Dude," Jay added, surprised.

"I told you to stay!" Carlos said to the dog.

"I flunked obedience class," said Dude matter-of-factly.

Jay smirked and rolled his eyes. "Great. And he can still talk."

Carlos lifted Dude from the trunk. "Lucky I love you. Come on."

Jay slammed the trunk shut.

"Oh, let me see," Mal said, and Carlos handed the fake wand to her. "Wow." She looked it over closely, then handed it back to Carlos. "This is great. Thank you so much." Then she turned to her friends. "All right, are we ready?"

Everyone nodded solemnly.

"Yeah." Evie held up Mal's backpack, which contained the smoke bombs.

"Let's do this." Mal purposefully turned and led her friends into the pipe tunnel.

Carlos turned back to Dude, pointing the fake wand at him. "Stay! I mean it!"

Dude, who was seated beside the limo, wagged his tail.

Then Carlos vanished into the pipe tunnel to catch up with his friends.

Dude followed quietly behind him.

On the deck of the ship, Uma and Harry were by Ben's side.

Harry pointed his hook at Ben's neck, then watched his clock. It was seconds away from noon. There were pirates perched on the rigging and rails of the ship. In the crow's nest, Gil scanned the cliffs. Harry checked his clock again. The minute hand struck noon. Harry grinned, scanning the rock cliffs and the pirate-filled pier—a series of wooden torch-lit platforms and steps leading down to their pirate ship.

"Hey, guys! They're here!" Gil started to climb down from the crow's nest.

Sure enough, Mal, Evie, Jay, Carlos, and Lonnie emerged from the rusty pipe tunnel that came out of the cliffside, and marched across a bridge that connected the pipe to the pier. Mal was leading, followed by Evie, Jay, Lonnie, and then Carlos.

They walked down the steps, passing pirates who strolled by or fished or hung up clothing on lines to dry. Wooden signs that said things like HOOK'S INLET, THIEVES' MARKET, and MISERY ROCK pointed every which way, and alligator-infested waters frothed below them in the dark mist. The pirate ship was waiting.

Uma turned to her crew and smiled wickedly. "Let's get this party started."

CHAPTER NINETEEN

THIS SITUATION COULD END UP BEING A *REAL* SHIPWRECK. BUT NOT WITH THE DAUGHTER OF MALEFICENT ON BOARD. NOW, LET'S TRICK THIS WITCH.

Mal reached the bridge that connected the pier to the pirate ship.

It was a rickety old thing, encrusted with brine. Below, sharp rocks and broken boardwalk beams jutted out of the roiling sea. Mal's friends stood behind her in a supportive huddle. In front of her, on the ship, were dozens of ragtag pirates, made fierce by face paint and glinting swords. Uma clung to Ben's arm. He stood on a plank with both hands behind his back, bound tightly with rope. Ben looked at Mal, whose eyes narrowed at Uma. Mal stepped onto the bridge.

She was going to get Ben back.

It would be the wand for the crown.

Harry stepped onto the bridge in front of Mal and glowered.

Uma strolled onto the bridge beside him, flipped back her long turquoise hair, and cackled. Harry's eyes bulged as he mumbled to Mal about what he'd do to harm Ben. In his excitement, he swung his sharp hook, but Uma grabbed it and yanked him back onto the ship. This trade would be between her and Mal.

Mal backed up, and Carlos shoved the fake wand into her hand.

At that instant, Harry tipped Ben forward on the plank. He gripped Ben by the jacket so that if he let go, Ben would surely plummet into the dark icy sea.

Mal and her friends froze and looked on, horror-struck.

Ben called out to Uma, telling her that he'd give her a chance at life in Auradon.

Uma met his offer with raucous laughter. Either Mal made the trade, she said, or Ben walked the plank. Uma walked farther out onto the bridge toward Mal, eying the sparkly wand gripped in her closed fist.

"Hold up," Uma commanded.

Mal waited.

"Too easy." Uma grinned. "Give it a test drive! We want to see it work."

The pirates behind her on the ship jeered and exchanged smiles.

Mal rolled her eyes. "Wow, you always were such a drama queen."

Uma's grin vanished. She sheathed her sword. "Nothing too big," she threatened, "or else Ben is fish bait."

Harry lowered Ben by his jacket even more.

"We're dead," Carlos muttered to his friends. But then Evie leaned in and whispered something to Carlos: "Dude."

Mal spun around to look at her friends in terror; then Carlos nodded to the side, toward where Dude was sitting on the pier. "Okay," said Mal, turning. She pointed the fake wand at Dude. *Although it seems absurd, turn your bark into a word!* Mal incanted.

Dude stared at her.

It was quiet except for the crashing of the tumultuous sea.

Mal and Uma glared at each other until Mal wheeled on Dude. "Talk, dog!"

Carlos gave Dude a squeeze to get him going.

"What? I hate public speaking!" cried Dude.

Uma's face broke into a smile, and the leering pirates behind her nodded and nudged one another, beaming and mumbling among themselves excitedly.

Mal and her friends exchanged tense looks.

Hook, line, and sinker? Mal wondered.

"Anyone have some bacon? Anyone?" Dude asked.

Uma turned toward Mal, revealing that her smile had been replaced by a wicked snarl. "Okay, give me the wand!" Uma barked. She put out her palm.

Mal drew the fake wand toward herself. "Give me Ben!" she shouted back at Uma.

Uma turned to Harry, who was still holding Ben over the side of the plank. "Let's go, Harry. Let's go!"

Disappointed, Harry yanked Ben off the plank and dragged him toward the bridge.

"Ben!" called Gil. "Before you go! Um . . . can you tell your mom that my dad says hi, and also, tell your dad that my dad says that he wishes he had gotten rid of your dad when he had the chance?"

Ben just looked at Gil as Harry continued to nudge him along.

"Come on!" Uma shouted.

Things happened in quick succession next. Once they reached Mal, Harry kicked Ben to his knees and drew his sword. Uma held out her hand for the wand again. Mal held out her hand for Ben.

"Cut him loose," Uma commanded Harry.

"I never get to have any fun," Harry complained as he sliced Ben free with his sword.

Ben grabbed Mal's hand, but as he started to stand, Uma put a hand on Ben's shoulder, letting him know he shouldn't get up so fast—not until she had what was owed to her. Uma bore daggers into Mal's eyes.

Mal handed the fake wand to her.

Uma couldn't help grinning once she had the wand in her possession.

Ben quickly leaped up beside Mal, and they slunk off the bridge.

Uma retreated to the ship, where the other pirates

swarmed around her and celebrated their victory with cheerful growls. She pointed the fake wand high overhead. *"By the power of the sea, tear it down and set us free!"* she incanted.

She thrust the wand at the magical barrier as the pirates grinned and roared.

Nothing happened.

Uma's smile faded.

"No!" Uma screamed, realizing she had been tricked. She broke the fake wand in two. "You do *not* get to win every time!" she yelled at Mal and her friends, who were halfway up the pier. Uma regarded her crew. "Get them!"

"Now!" yelled Mal.

Carlos used his slingshot to launch a smoke bomb, which exploded in a thick colorful cloud.

The pirates ducked and fell back but were quickly up again.

Carlos chucked another smoke bomb.

"Go!" Uma commanded her pirates.

They roared in anger and swarmed past Uma, who stood furiously glowering at Mal and her friends.

Jay tipped a barrel that stowed the quiver of

swords. He doled out swords to Evie, Lonnie, Mal, Ben, and Carlos. The friends took strong stances and braced themselves against the pirates, who were charging forward at full speed and swinging on ropes from the ship to the pier. They were out for blood.

In moments, Mal and her friends were battling the vicious crew.

Lonnie fought a pirate and disarmed him. Wanting a real fight, she said, "Here. Take mine," and offered her sword. The pirate grabbed it and struck at Lonnie. She ducked out of the way once, twice, three times, four times and kicked the pirate, who flew backward onto a landing. Then she picked up her sword, thrust it in the pirate's direction to scare him, laughed, and ran, leaving him groveling on the floor.

Harry had leaped from the ship onto a ladder and landed facing Jay on the pier. He removed his pirate's hat and twirled his hair, sizing Jay up. He unsheathed his sword and swung. Jay dodged the blade. Soon Harry was swinging his hook, too. They parried and thrust, blade hitting blade. Harry pinned Jay against a wooden rail with his hook and sword locked on to Jay's sword, and Harry's pirate's hat fell into the sea below. In a few snakelike moves, Jay freed himself from the tangle, and he kicked Harry down while yanking his hook right off his hand. Jay dangled the hook off his sword blade and held it out over the edge of the boardwalk, smiling. Harry extended his hand, but Jay let the hook slide off his blade and fall into the sea. Harry moved past him, ducked under the rail, and dove in after it.

Being the captain of R.O.A.R. had come in handy.

Meanwhile, Mal had been knocking pirates' swords away with hers while Evie and Carlos did the same. Mal sent one pirate flying off the bridge and into the sea. She dodged a few more and ducked under others. *I've still got it,* she thought.

Finally, Uma strolled across the bridge toward her.

It was time for the two of them to battle now.

CHAPTER TWENTY

O H, PLEASE. UMA SHOULD KNOW ALL ABOUT BAD DEALS. HER MOM IS URSULA, FOR BADNESS' SAKE!

Uma swung her sword at Mal with every bit of strength she had.

Mal blocked it with hers, again and again. Their blades quivered against each other, and their panting faces were inches apart, much like during their arm wrestling match—but the loser of this struggle would not live to spill the tea about it later.

"Hi!" Mal pressed her face closer to Uma's. "Didja miss me?" She smiled.

Uma sneered as she struck her sword against Mal's.

Chop!

Chop!

Chop!

"Come on!" Uma roared.

Mal and Uma swung swords. Blade hit blade. Their weapons collided in a perfect X—locked there, trembling. Uma grabbed Mal's forearm and pushed her backward, then pushed off her and spun, only to face her again. Uma swung, and Mal stomped on her blade and ground it under her boot, then ran up the steps. Uma followed right behind her, pirate sword poised in her hand.

"Uma!" cried Harry from the edge of the dock. He was dripping wet, holding the hook he had recovered.

Uma knelt and took her friend's hand, helping him drag his drenched body onto the dry wharf. Then she quickly turned back toward the melee. "Mal's mine!" She took off with Harry following her hungrily.

Ahead, Gil swung at Ben, pinning him to the floorboards until Carlos interfered. Ben ducked and rolled under their crossed swords and ran off, and Carlos battled Gil. He snatched up a dented old bucket and shoved it down over Gil's head. Then Carlos took Gil's sword and tapped the blade against the side of the bucket before kicking Gil off the boardwalk entirely. Carlos laughed at his victory.

Evie fought another pirate. She blocked his sword with hers. "Nice scarf!" she cried as she yanked it off his neck and he spun to the floor. "It's mine now!" While Ben leaped beside Evie and sword-fought with his own pirate, Evie dueled yet another one, disarming him—and herself accidentally. She threw a basket at him, and he flew back and out of sight. "That's the way you do it, boys," she said with a winning smile.

Carlos shouted from the top of the pier, "Jay, start the car!"

Jay and Lonnie ran across the bridge and vanished into the pipe tunnel.

"Mal, come on!" Evie called to her friend.

Mal bolted up more steps of the multi-level pier until she finally reached the top and found herself face-to-face with Ben. "Ben!" she cried. "Ben, go!"

Ben pulled Mal close. "I'm not leaving you. If we're going down, we're going down together!"

The tender moment was cut short. A drenched Harry, wielding his hook, leaped onto the platform and swung his sword at Ben, who ducked behind a ladder, grabbed Harry's arm, and held him in place. Then Ben tickled Harry's chin in a mocking way.

"Coochy coochy coo," said Ben.

Harry lunged at Ben with his hook, but Ben moved out of the way.

Uma and Gil raced up the steps, and Uma charged Mal, grinning maniacally. All her teeth showed. She struck Mal's sword again and again, with great agility and surprising strength, but Mal kept blocking her, nearly buckling under the blows.

"Say your prayers, sweetie!" Uma stabbed at her.

Mal swung back. "You got something between your teeth!" she called out, trying to distract her opponent.

"Feels like old times, eh?" Uma told Mal with a smile. They swung at each other in a lethal dance. They spun, hair twirling wildly. "Only this time you lose!" Uma slashed at Mal again and again, her hair flying out from under her pirate's hat, her eyes intense and her mouth set in a snarl. Finally, Uma's sword connected with Mal's leg. Her leather pants ripped. Mal cried out. Uma glared at her and went in for the kill.

Meanwhile, Harry charged Ben, about to strike.

It looked like all was lost for Mal and her friends.

Just then, Evie chucked a smoke bomb.

A purple cloud exploded, and all the pirates backed away, spluttering.

It was just the diversion the friends needed.

"Let's go! Come on!" Evie grabbed Ben. The two of them ran across the bridge and into the pipe tunnel after Carlos, with Mal in step behind them.

Mal spun around in the entrance to the tunnel. Uma ran up and stopped short of the bridge. Mal looked across it into Uma's eyes, and she grinned. Then, with a kick of her boot, Mal broke the piece of the bridge that connected it to the pipe tunnel. The bridge fell and dangled uselessly from an old chain.

Mal smirked at Uma triumphantly. Then Mal walked away, vanishing into the darkness of the tunnel. Across the divide, Uma glared haughtily, panting hard. She wheeled around, shouted, and marched past her crew to the ship.

Uma hadn't been this mad since Ben had invited Mal and her friends to Auradon. *The battle may be won, but the war is far from over,* she thought angrily.

Not far from the limo, Dude emerged from the pipe tunnel into the alley, followed by Carlos and Evie.

They hurried into the limo.

Ben ran out of the tunnel next, then spun around. "Mal!" he called. His voice echoed off the rusty walls of the tunnel. He extended a hand into the darkness. Mal took it and stepped into the alley, and she and Ben rushed to the limo.

"Come on, come on, come on!" Lonnie urged Mal and Ben, who hurriedly tossed their swords into the trunk and climbed into the vehicle. Ben immediately shut the door. Lonnie slammed the trunk and raced to the passenger seat, and the limo peeled out.

As they quickly sped through the streets of the Isle of the Lost, Mal turned around in her seat in a panic, realizing too late that she had dropped something as she hurried into the limo.

"My Spell Book!"

CHAPTER TWENTY-ONE

I COULDN'T BELIEVE I'D LEFT MY SPELL BOOK BEHIND. I ALSO COULDN'T BELIEVE I WAS HEADED BACK TO AURADON.

Ben and Mal were still trying to catch their breath. They sat side by side, but with an empty seat between them.

"I'm really sorry that things didn't turn out the way you wanted," said Ben.

Mal turned to look at him. She didn't know what to say. "I mean, as long as you're safe, that's . . ." Her voice trailed off and she looked away.

A tiny smile formed on Ben's face. "At least I finally got to see the Isle. They're my people, too," he said. "*Uma* helped me see that."

Mal looked back at Ben, staring in disbelief. "Ben. Uma *captured* you."

"She's an angry girl . . . with a bad plan. Not so

different from *you* when you came to Auradon, Mal."

Ouch. Mal looked away, stung.

Ben faced the window.

"Awkward," said Dude.

Evie and Carlos exchanged glances.

"Dude, I know you can speak, but it doesn't always mean you should," Carlos told him.

"Here we go!" called Jay from the driver's seat of the limo.

He aimed the remote out the front window, and the limo blasted through the magical barrier in a blinding flash of light and emerged on the other side. Everyone let out sighs of relief. Jay loosened his grip on the wheel, and Lonnie smiled at him from the passenger seat.

Jay sighed, then turned to Lonnie. "Why don't you stop by practice later?"

"In the mood to break some rules?" asked Lonnie, recalling the R.O.A.R. rule about a captain and eight men.

"No." Jay's eyebrows furrowed; then he quickly smiled.

Soon the limo pulled past the sign outside the school.

WELCOME TO AURADON PREP.

GOODNESS DOESN'T GET ANY BETTER.

After Jay parked the limo back in its spot, the five teens made their way across the sunny campus.

Mal walked silently with Ben at the back of the group, with Evie, Carlos, and Dude in front of them and Jay and Lonnie in the lead.

Lonnie carried the quiver of swords. "I'll get these back to the gym."

"Yeah, thanks," said Jay.

Lonnie grinned at him, and her eyes twinkled. "See you later." She dashed off.

Jane ran up to Ben, wielding her trusty tablet. "Ben! There you are. Cotillion's tonight!"

She pulled him away from Mal and showed him the tablet. "This is the stained glass window for Mal. Isn't it beautiful? She's going to love it!" Jane squealed.

"Hold on," Ben told Jane. He spoke to Mal. "Do you want to cancel?"

Mal looked up at Ben and her mouth opened.

Jane looked from Ben to Mal. "Oh! I can come back. But, you know, like really, really soon."

"No, no, no. Now's fine," said Ben, turning back to Jane. Then, after a beat, he leaned in toward Mal, put a hand on her lower back, and whispered, "Do whatever you need to do." He gave Mal one last long glance and walked away with Jane to talk last-minute details for the event.

Evie took Mal by the arm. "We need to talk," Evie told her, starting to walk.

Carlos cut in. "No," he said.

Evie and Mal turned around to face him.

"*No?*" Evie asked Carlos.

"No," he said. "You guys are always going off in a huddle, whispering all your girl-talk stuff, or whatever, and Jay and I are tired of it." He looked at Jay.

"I'm not," said Jay.

Carlos ignored him. "We're your family, too," he told Mal. "We've been through a lot together. We're not stopping now. So everybody *sit*." Carlos sat on the grass with Dude in his lap. Jay sat down next to him. Evie and Mal sat, too.

"I don't actually know how to start girl talk." Carlos's eyes shifted.

Mal and Evie giggled uncomfortably.

"Whaddup?" Jay said in an attempt to break the ice.

Everyone looked at each other.

"Well . . ." Mal started.

Her friends looked at her.

Mal looked back at them. "I'm a mess," she confessed, beginning to cry. "Six months ago, I was stealing candy from babies, and now . . . everybody wants me to be the lady of the court. And I can't keep up with the act."

"Then don't," said Carlos.

"See? This was dumb." Jay planted his hands in the grass and moved to stand.

"Maybe it wasn't," said Evie.

Jay sank back down.

Evie took Mal's hand. "We're always going to be

the kids from the Isle. I tried to forget it, but those are our roots. And we all did what we had to do to survive. But it made us who we are. And we're never going to be like anybody else here. And that's okay."

"And we can't fake it," added Carlos.

"Yeah, especially without my spell book," said Mal.

"If Ben doesn't love the real you, he's not the one," said Carlos.

Evie agreed. She looked at Mal. "I like that."

"Give him a chance," Carlos said.

"I'm going to make some changes to your dress," Evie told her. "And if you're up for it—only if you're up for it—it'll be waiting for you, okay?"

Evie released Mal's hand, grabbed her bag, and walked off with the boys.

But then Jay hung back and plopped down in front of Mal. "Come to Cotillion tonight. If Ben isn't smart enough to love you, and you can't stand another day, I'll drive you back tomorrow myself."

Mal just looked at Jay. He rested a hand on her shoulder, stood, and strolled off. Alone, Mal stared into the distance. If only she knew what her heart was telling her to do. She had known before. Why didn't she this time?

Or maybe she did.

CHAPTER TWENTY-TWO

AS EVERYONE GETS READY FOR COTILLION, I'LL JUST BE QUIETLY FREAKING OUT....

Carlos and Dude walked on the grassy school lawn toward the dorms.

There were groups of students in pastel-colored Auradon Prep clothes standing in clumps, chatting with others, and strolling to class in the shade of trees.

"*Girl talk*. Crushed it," said Dude.

Carlos laughed. "Yeah, except when it comes to asking Jane out. Then I'm a total chicken," he said.

"I'm going to paraphrase one of the bravest boys I know," said Dude.

Carlos stopped and looked down at him, waiting for the rest.

Dude cleared his throat. "If she doesn't like you, then she's not the one for you."

Carlos knelt down, smiling. "You really are man's best friend." He scratched the top of Dude's head, then laughed and stood up. "Come on, buddy, let's go."

Jay was wearing his sporty blue-and-yellow R.O.A.R. outfit when he strolled into the amphitheater, where the team had assembled. They were in the arena, stretching.

"Let's bring it in!" Jay clapped.

Everyone gathered around him.

"All right," Jay said. "You all know I come from the Isle, all right, where things are pretty wack. But there is one thing the Isle's got on Auradon: if you're strong, we want you by our side—girl or boy."

Chad stepped beside him. "Hold on here, Jay. We don't break rules here in Auradon, okay? That's more on the Isle."

Jay pulled the rule book from his pocket and read from it. " 'The team shall be comprised of *a captain* and eight men.' So, uh, give it up for your new team captain." He pocketed the rule book and turned to the doorway, where Lonnie appeared in a custom-designed pink-and-teal R.O.A.R. uniform. She quickly joined the guys.

Jay placed a whistle around her neck, bowed, and left her in the center. Then he clapped, which started a chain reaction of applause throughout the rest of the team. Everyone but Chad put his hands together. Then Jay led the team in a unified bow, and everyone bowed to Lonnie except for Chad. Lonnie looked long and hard at him, and he finally gave in and bowed along with the others.

Lonnie was ready for her new role. She blew her whistle. "Give me ten!" she instructed. "Come on, guys!"

The boys dropped for push-ups and began to count.

Lonnie put a foot on Chad's back. "Pick it up, Chad!" she said. "Nice form, Jay!"

Jay smiled at her and went lower into his push-up, showing how strong he really was.

Lonnie laughed, took a step back, and blew her whistle again. " 'Kay, practice is over," she said to her team. "Get outta here! Go get ready for Cotillion."

The team dispersed and jogged out of the amphitheater.

"Hey, Jay!" said Lonnie from the arena.

He turned and walked over to her. "Yeah?"

Lonnie smiled. "Wait till I tell my mom."

Jay smiled and gave her a playful tap on the shoulder. "Let's get outta here."

Inside Mal and Evie's dorm room, Evie was altering Mal's dress.

She gathered up bits of fabric and swaths of gold lamé and glanced at the pile of Dizzy's hair creations. She took a headband, turned it over in her hands, and added a piece of leather. It was just the touch the headband needed. She smiled.

Doug knocked on the open door, then entered before Evie could answer. He was pale. "I have a scout badge in s'mores!" he cried. "How could you go camping without me? Are you seeing someone else?" He was so upset his mouth trembled.

"*What?* No!" said Evie.

"Is it Happy's son?" asked Doug, taking another step into the room. "Let me tell you, he isn't as happy as his dad. Kind of a dark streak, in fact."

Evie took his hands and gave him her full attention. "Ben was taken on the Isle. We rescued him and saved Auradon."

"So . . . you're not seeing anyone else?" asked Doug, relieved.

Evie laughed. "Don't be dopey."

Doug smiled. Dopey might've been his dad, but Doug was his own person.

"Come on," said Evie, "we've got dresses to deliver." She looked at the headband, and her eyes lit up. "And that's not all." She looked back at Doug. "*I've* been given a chance, and now I need to give someone else a chance, too."

"My uncle Bashful used to say that. But really quietly," said Doug.

Evie gathered up Dizzy's hair accessories, smiled at Doug, and headed out. "Let's do this," she said.

〜〜

Out on the lawn, Carlos saw Jane hurrying with her tablet and talking on the phone. She was wearing her Auradon Prep blue, white, and yellow cheerleading uniform.

Carlos quickly ran up to her and grinned.

Jane smiled at him and lowered her phone.

Before he could lose his nerve, Carlos just came out with it: "Uh . . . would you . . . go to Cotillion with me?" he asked.

Jane didn't get it. "We're all taking a stretch carriage over at six," she explained. Then she went back to her phone call. "Yeah, no, no. The pen toppers on the left side."

"No, I mean, uh . . . with *me*." Carlos pointed to himself.

"I'll stop by your room," she said, still not comprehending. Then Jane spoke back into her phone. "No, no, no. So when you're on the boat facing the left—Yeah, yeah, right. No, no, no, not *right*—left!"

"Uh . . ." said Carlos, getting her attention again. "This is gonna be trickier than I thought," he mumbled to himself. "Jane?"

"Yeah?"

He put a hand on her phone and slowly lowered it. "Would you . . . be my date for Cotillion? And if you don't hate me by the end of it, would you consider . . . maybe being more than friends . . . maybe?" He looked at her with widening eyes, waiting.

Jane's face broke into a huge smile. "Like . . . *boyfriend and girlfriend*? Where we hold hands instead of slugging each other all the time? And we text? And I can tell you how great you are? Because, Carlos, you're really . . . you're so great. And you're so cute and so nice and I'm the luckiest girl in the world!" She hopped up and down.

"Me too!" said Carlos. "I mean, *guy!*"

"No, right!" said Jane.

"Luckiest *guy!*" said Carlos.

Jane gave him a big hug.

"Oh!" said Carlos. It took him a second to register what was happening before he hugged her back.

Jane's phone buzzed, and she broke apart from him. "Oh! Sorry!" She held up her phone. She was grinning at him. "I'll see you later?" she asked Carlos.

"Yeah. Totally," he said.

He watched her pass through the rows of hedges, back up toward the school.

Dude's tail wagged. "Good boy," he said to Carlos. Carlos laughed and patted him. "Come on, Dude. Let's go."

In the boys' dorm room, Chad pulled a crown from Carlos's 3-D printer.

He wore his baby-blue suit with gold details and the amazing faux-fur-trimmed cape Evie had designed for him. He added the fake crown to the regal ensemble and admired himself in the mirror. "Not bad. Not bad at all. What's that? Why no, Audrey, I haven't chosen my queen yet." He turned away from the mirror, wheeled back to face it, and winked at his reflection.

Just then, Chad's cell phone rang. He walked to the table and saw the screen. It was Audrey calling. He picked up the phone, fumbled it, dropped it on the floor, and dove for it. *"Audrey!"* he exclaimed.

Carlos appeared in the doorway. "Chad, this is—"

"Sh! Sh!" hissed Chad from the floor.

"*My* room," finished Carlos.

Chad held up a finger as he listened to his phone. "Audrey? Yeah?" He got up on his knees. "Oh, that's wonderful!" Chad turned to Carlos. "She's got a flat tire in Sherwood Forest, and she wants *me* to go change it!" He stood up and chuckled.

Carlos squinted at him. "That's *six* hours away."

"Just six?" Chad spoke into the phone: "I'm going to be there sooner than I thought!" He sauntered toward the doorway.

Carlos stopped him. "Uh . . ." He removed Chad's crown. "My printer, my crown. Thank you."

Chad realized he wasn't going to win this one. He glared at Carlos as he passed him, then said, "Coming, Audrey!" He sprinted down the hall.

"Wow." Carlos scoffed.

CHAPTER TWENTY-THREE

COTILLION. IT'S TIME.
   I HAVE A MILLION THOUGHTS IN MY HEAD BUT JUST ONE
FEELING IN MY HEART.
   AND I HOPE MY HEART IS RIGHT.

The only event grander than Ben's coronation ceremony was Cotillion.

For starters, it was being held on a sleek white party yacht called *True Love* that was docked in the marina. Auradon royal crests adorned either side of the yacht. Orbs of light hung from long cables strung over the deck. There were little round tables with lamps on them here and there, leaving plenty of room for people to dance. A set of stairs with a blue-and-gold-trimmed carpet led up to a stage. Everything looked incredible.

Partygoers boarded the yacht in front of roped-off fans and paparazzi, and a few, including Evie and Doug, stopped to talk with news reporters in front of the step and repeat. Evie wore a floor-length midnight-blue dress with black beading branching across it, a long blue cape, red gloves, and a thin gold choker featuring a red heart gem centerpiece. Her handbag was the shape of a poison apple with a bite taken out of it. And to top it all off, she wore Dizzy's ruby-studded hair ornament clipped neatly to the side of her bun. Evie struck pose after pose for the cameras.

News reporters held microphones up to her. "Evie, you look beautiful!"

"Thank you," said Evie.

"The dress is gorgeous! Did you design the barrette?"

"No, it's not my creation, actually," she said. "Many of the hair accessories this evening are by a fabulous new designer, *Dizzy of the Isle!*"

"Who's your date?"

"*This* is my Doug." Evie extended a hand, and Doug took it and moved closer to her. "Dopey's son."

He stood by her in his tan suit and black bow tie and waved.

Meanwhile, on the Isle, at Lady Tremaine's Curl Up and Dye, Dizzy watched the live feed from the Cotillion on a boxy old TV. After Evie's mention of her hair accessories, Dizzy shrieked.

"I made that! That's *me!*" She squealed again with glee.

Lady Tremaine banged the floor above her, as if to say *shut it.*

Dizzy put a hand to her mouth and flinched at the sound. "Sorry, Granny!" She spun back around to face the TV. She couldn't help smiling.

Jane and Carlos descended the steps to the party deck, past bushels of colorful flowers in clusters of white, yellow, and blue, toward the table where people served fruit punch. Carlos was super fashionable, as usual, in red knee-length pants and a black-and-white leather jacket. Jane's gown was a long sparkling periwinkle dress with a magenta bow at the waist.

When Fairy Godmother spotted Jane with Carlos, her face lit up. "Jane! Jane, there you are, my dear one!" She made her way from the refreshments table to the dance floor, waving her magic wand and looking like a true fairy in a pale blue dress and hooded cape tied at the neck with a pale silk bow. "Everything looks beautiful, my love, but we need to ladle out the punch before the sherbet melts."

"Mom," said Jane.

Fairy Godmother looked at her expectantly.

"I have a date," said Jane with a smile.

Fairy Godmother gasped and grinned. "A *date*?"

Jane nodded.

"*Really!*" Fairy Godmother looked at Carlos, then over the deck, searching.

Carlos awkwardly looked around.

Fairy Godmother rested a hand on his shoulder. "Do you have a date, too?"

"Yeah." He gestured to Jane.

"Really!" said Fairy Godmother with a smile.

Carlos laughed. "Yeah."

Fairy Godmother looked around again, not quite getting it.

"Mom." Jane took Carlos's hands.

Fairy Godmother looked down at their intertwined hands. Then she looked up from Jane to Carlos, realizing. "Bibbidi-bobbidi! *Ooh!*" she said with a great big smile.

Carlos let out a little laugh. He looked Jane in the eyes and nodded toward the dance floor. "After you."

Jane walked off with Carlos, and they danced on the deck. He spun her and then kissed her hand. Evie and Doug were dancing there, too, along with Jay, who boogied with a group of girls. Jay looked handsome in his red-and-gold leather suit jacket and crimson fingerless gloves. The girls swooned. He moved to dance with Lonnie, whose dress was actually a coral pink jumpsuit with a long open skirt.

The music stopped, getting everyone's attention. Young men in pale yellow suits lined the yacht's steps, and in one unified motion they lifted their trumpets and began playing fanfare.

All eyes turned to Lumiere at the top of the steps. He had thin gray hair and resembled the candelabrum he had once been enchanted to be. That night he wore a white suit with gold epaulets and a pale gold bow tie. "The future . . . *Lady Mal!*" Lumiere announced.

Mal entered at the top of the staircase.

She looked stunning in her yellow dress bejeweled with blue gems, blue and yellow tulle, and a sparkling cape that trailed the ground behind her. Evie had edged up the look, adding a leather bracelet, boots, and a crown-esque hair ornament. Mal's purple hair was in a pretty side braid that snaked down her shoulder. She looked down at all the people silently watching her from the ship's deck. Mal's heartbeat quickened. The throng responded to Mal's purple hair with a murmur of surprise, which was drowned out by Mal's friends, who clapped and cheered. Others joined in. Photographers turned all their video equipment on Mal.

Lumiere joined Mal at her side. "Work it, girl," he whispered.

Mal giggled. She surveyed the crowd again.

Where is Ben?

Then she descended the steps toward the deck as everyone applauded.

Belle and Beast greeted Mal at the bottom of the stairs. Beast, in his royal-blue suit with gold sash and signature black bold-frame glasses, took Mal's trembling hand.

"Hi," said Mal, comforted by him.

"Ben's on his way," said Beast. "You look beautiful."

Belle wore a gold dress and a delicate crystal-encrusted gold crown. She also took Mal's hand and smiled lovingly. "So beautiful," she said. "I know we were shocked at first, but you—you were exactly what Ben needs." She was referring to the Family Day event, when Ben had first announced to Belle and Beast that Mal was his new girlfriend. The photographer had captured their shocked expressions upon hearing the news.

Beast gave Belle a little side hug. "And lucky for me, she doesn't go by first impressions," he said. He, Belle, and Mal laughed, though Mal's laugh was nervous.

Evie could sense that Mal was apprehensive. In true best-friend fashion, Evie rushed to her side. "Hi!" She led Mal onto the deck. "How are you feeling?"

Mal looked at the cameras and guests. "I feel like I'm going to throw up."

"It's okay. We're here with you," said Evie.

Mal grabbed Evie's hands. More fanfare played. It was a great moment for the VKs. Mal and Evie beamed at each other.

Lumiere called out, "King Benjamin!"

Ben appeared at the top of the stairs in a sleek royal-blue silk jacket with gold accents. The belt he wore had a gold beast-emblem buckle. His honey-brown hair was swept across his forehead under his thick gold crown, and his blue eyes sparkled like stars. He looked every bit a king.

Everyone applauded. Mal couldn't take her eyes off him. Ben nodded, and his eyes met Mal's. She smiled at him. He walked down the stairs and paused at the bottom.

"Go get him," Evie whispered to Mal.

Mal took a step forward.

Ben passed his parents without looking their way.

Okay . . . Belle mouthed to Beast at the slight.

Ben stopped in front of Mal and bowed.

Mal bowed back at him.

"Mal," said Ben, coming up from his bow, "I wish

I had time to explain. . . ." He turned around and looked toward the top of the stairs.

Mal smiled.

Could this have something to do with all those not-so-secret discussions Ben has been having with Jane? wondered Mal.

Then her eyes widened and her jaw dropped. The crowd gasped in shock.

CHAPTER TWENTY-FOUR

U MA? HERE AT COTILLION?
YEAH, I'M OFFICIALLY GOING TO BE SICK. AND NOT
BECAUSE I'M ON A BOAT.

Uma glowed in a teal-and-gold mermaid-style dress
as she entered the grand staircase.

Her gown was simply exquisite, with tiers of
sea-colored tulle and delicate nets threaded into the
pieces of the fabric. Her hair was up in a bun, and she
wore dark fingerless gloves and carried a turquoise
clutch. Her gold shell necklace shimmered against
her chest. Uma smiled kindly at Ben and walked
down the steps to meet him.

Ben kissed his beast-head ring on Uma's finger.

Mal looked on with tear-filled eyes.

Ben linked his arm with Uma's and led her to Mal. "I'm sorry. It all happened so fast," Ben told Mal.

Mal stared at him.

"Something happened to me when I was on the Isle with Uma." Ben looked at Uma dreamily. "A connection."

Uma giggled at him.

Mal shook her head. "I'm sorry . . . what are you saying?"

"I'm saying that—" Ben began.

"It was love!" Uma smiled at Mal. "I just—I realized how alike Ben and I are, you know?"

"We are," said Ben.

"I know!" Uma beamed.

Mal looked back at Ben. "Ben."

Uma giggled and pulled Ben close.

"Ben," Mal said a little louder.

He looked at her.

"Did you go *back* for her?" Mal asked.

"He didn't have to," said Uma. "I dove through the barrier before it closed. And I'm an excellent swimmer, so . . . Listen, Mal. I just want to say thank you. I really do." She giggled again. "For everything.

Just . . . thank you." She threw her arms theatrically around Mal and gave her a tight-as-tentacles strong embrace that made Mal recoil.

"Don't you see, Mal?" said Ben. "You were right! See? You knew that we weren't meant to be together. That's why you never told me that you loved me. Thank you."

Mal stared at him. She had no words.

Uma beamed at Ben, who had a glazed expression on his face. They joined together and waltzed across the deck. Evie led a stunned Mal away from them.

Mal was shaken, and she couldn't take her eyes off Ben. Carlos held one of her arms and Evie held the other, for support. They watched as Uma and Ben danced a Cotillion waltz in front of the surprised crowd.

"Not too thrilled I risked my life for him," Carlos said bitterly.

Lonnie joined them. "Well, we're with you, Mal." She rested a hand on Mal's arm.

Jay walked over, too. "Let's get out of here. Come on."

The crowd quickly cleared a path for them as they

headed toward the stairs to leave. Beast and Belle gasped as they watched Mal being led out.

"Mal!" cried Beast, stopping her.

"We're so sorry, honey, we had no idea," said Belle.

"I'm going to talk to him," Beast promised.

Suddenly, Jane raced up the steps toward Lumiere, who still stood at the top. "Lumiere! Lumiere! Unveil the gift! They need to see it! Now!" she shouted.

"And now, the unveiling of King Ben's masterpiece, designed especially for his lady," said Lumiere, signaling a guard across the deck to uncover the art piece as fanfare played.

Mal, Evie, Jay, Lonnie, and Carlos, now joined by Jane and Doug, froze on the steps.

Uma and Ben turned.

All eyes watched as the guard on the opposite landing pulled a cord. A royal-blue drape fell away, revealing the stained glass panel Ben had commissioned for Mal.

Mal's eyes filled with tears again.

CHAPTER TWENTY-FIVE

BEN DOES LOVE ME! HIS GIFT PROVES IT.
AND CRAZY AS IT SOUNDS, I LOVE HIM, TOO.

The stained glass panel depicted a sunrise with Ben and Mal.

On the right, Ben wore his royal-blue suit with gold epaulets and crown. He reached for Mal's hand. On the left, Mal, with long purple hair and a gold crown, wore a purple dress and cape that swept around her. It wasn't the perfect Lady of the Court Mal. Not at all. It depicted the real Mal, in all her purple-haired, green-eyed glory. The party guests applauded. Mal couldn't take her eyes off it. She knew Ben must have been planning and designing the stained glass panel for months. She couldn't believe her eyes.

Mal spoke to Evie. "*Ben* did that?"

"Yeah, he did," said Evie.

"Evie." Mal took her hand. "Ben has known who I was all along."

"And he loves the real you, M." Evie looked at her.

"A true love," said Mal, gazing at the portrait in awe.

"Yeah." Evie smiled.

"Told you," said Carlos.

Mal laughed.

Ben stared up at the stained glass, his vacant expression changing to one of contemplation.

Uma marched to the stairs. *"Cover that thing back up!"* she snarled.

"I will not!" proclaimed Lumiere.

Uma smiled and turned to face Ben. "Why don't you tell everyone the present you have for *me*, Ben?"

Ben approached the stairs. "I have an announcement!" he declared.

Beast removed his glasses and started to walk down the steps toward him.

"Uma will be joining the court tonight as my lady." He took Uma's hand.

Mal stared, speechless. *After all that?*

Uma beamed and chuckled.

Beast stepped onto the deck. *"Son!"* he boomed.

"Not now, Dad!" roared Ben in his most beast-like voice.

The crowd froze, scared.

Ben addressed his subjects. "So as my gift to her, I am bringing down the barrier once and for all!" He looked into Uma's eyes, and she beamed at him.

Mal and Evie gasped and looked at each other.

On the Isle of the Lost, Uma's pirate posse had the live feed of the Cotillion on the old television in the fish and chips shop. They watched as Lumiere announced Uma.

"Mateys," said Harry, standing at the counter. "We ride with the tide!"

The pirates cheered and whooped. They drummed on the table and kicked their legs up in the air and clapped their gloved hands and high-fived. Harry locked lips with Gil. The pirates danced, twirling triumphantly as if they were on the yacht.

Their time had come.

"Fairy Godmother, bring down the barrier!" Ben bellowed.

Fairy Godmother's mouth was a perfect circle. "I most certainly will not!" She gripped her wand tighter.

"I am your *king*," said Ben.

"Obey him," demanded Uma.

"Bring down the barrier!" Ben boomed.

Mal's eyes lit up. "You guys!" she whispered to her friends on the steps as they huddled up. "You guys! He's been spelled!"

"Uma found your spell book!" whispered Evie.

They turned and watched Ben take Uma's hand and gaze into her eyes.

Mal looked around. Her eye caught the image on the stained glass. Suddenly, she knew what to do. She stepped forward.

Mal faced Ben.

"*Ben!*" Mal smiled and stepped in front of him.

Everyone waited to see what would happen next.

"Ben! Look at me," Mal pleaded.

Ben turned toward her.

"No! Eyes over here!" Uma said, standing beside Mal. "You love me, remember?"

"No, you don't," Mal told him.

"Yes, you do!" Uma shouted.

"Ben, look at me," said Mal.

Uma turned toward Fairy Godmother. "Bring down the barrier!"

"I do *not* take orders from you," said Fairy Godmother.

"Ben!" Uma commanded.

Ben continued looking at Mal, transfixed now.

Mal took step after step, closing the space between them. "Ben, I never told you I loved you because I didn't believe that I was good enough, and I thought that it was only a matter of time before you saw that yourself—"

"Oh, please." Uma rolled her eyes.

Mal pointed at the stained glass. "But, Ben, that's me! I'm part Isle and I'm part Auradon—"

"Ben, eyes over here." Uma smiled.

Mal's eyes filled with tears. "And you saw us for who we were and who we can be—"

"You love *me*," Uma interjected.

"And, Ben . . . I know what love feels like now," said Mal.

"Don't listen to her, Ben. Don't listen to her," said Uma.

"But, Ben, of course I love you. Of course I love you. I've always loved you." Mal kissed him.

Uma stepped back and looked on.

Then Mal pulled away and gazed up into Ben's eyes, which suddenly seemed clear.

Ben smiled at Mal. "My Mal."

"True Love's Kiss," said Evie to herself, grinning. "Works every time."

The crowd cheered.

Uma lunged at Fairy Godmother. "Give me that wand!"

Fairy Godmother yanked it out of reach. "Ah-ah-ah." She called out for the guards. "Seize her!"

The crowd swarmed Uma, but she quickly ran to the railing.

Mal held up her arms to block the guards. "No! No! No! Stop!" As much as she wasn't fond of Uma,

Mal felt in her heart that jailing her was not the answer.

Uma backed against the rail and faced Mal and the rest of her onlookers.

"Uma, I know you. You are so much more than just a villain," said Mal. "And you have to believe me, because I have been there. Do not let your pride get in the way of something that you really want." Mal took a step toward Uma, then another. "Yeah?"

Uma looked at Mal and touched her shell necklace, which had started to glow. Then she turned, put her hand on the rail, and stepped up onto the banister.

Mal ran forward to stop her.

Everyone behind her screamed and rushed forward as well.

But it was too late.

Uma leaped off the yacht.

Everyone raced to the railing, including Mal, whose mouth was agape. Ben's eyes bugged. Carlos, Jay, Lonnie, Jane, the guards, and the rest of the party guests looked at each other, murmuring. All of a sudden, they saw a slight bubbling in the sea below that turned into a roiling boil, and then . . . and then . . .

Out of the waves, Uma rose as an enormous tentacled sea witch.

CHAPTER TWENTY-SIX

TALK ABOUT GOING OVERBOARD! SHRIMPY JUST GOT A WHOLE LOT BIGGER.

GUESS THE SLIMY TENTACLE DOESN'T FALL FAR FROM THE SEA WITCH.

Uma sloshed a wave of water over the yacht that sent everyone stumbling.

Then she vanished under the waves and resurfaced. "True Love's Kiss won't defeat *this*!" Uma roared, grinning. "The world *will* know my name!" She threw back her arms, then flung out long slimy tentacles. One nearly swept Evie into the sea, but she jumped aside. Another lashed out at Lonnie and Jane, who dodged it. Uma cackled with her hands on her hips; then she folded her arms, ready to strike again.

Mal watched her friends avoid Uma's attacks. She clenched her fists. Her eyes sparkled bright green, her hair whipped with magic, and then . . .

Mal vanished in a burst of purple smoke—and turned into a giant dragon.

She had iridescent purple scales and a bilious-green underbelly, razor-sharp claws and teeth, two curved horns on the top of her head, and a long spiked tail.

It would have made Maleficent a proud mom had she been there to see it.

Everyone on the yacht gasped.

Mal locked her glowing green eyes with those of the enormous sea witch.

"Bring it on, Mal!" Uma yelled, swiping with her arms and tentacles as Mal wheeled overhead. "Let's finish this—once and for all!"

Mal spread her huge green-purple wings and soared over Uma, breathing out flames. People on the yacht crouched down to evade the heat. Uma ducked under the waves, rocking the yacht violently back and forth, with everyone on deck staggering one way, then the other.

Ben had seen enough. He roared mightily, removed his crown and jacket, and ran to the banister. Despite the screams from the guests, Ben dove off the yacht into the sea. He surfaced between the two dueling giants. *"Stop!"* Ben shouted. "Mal! Uma! Back down!" He looked from one massive monster to the other. "Back down!"

Mal and Uma broke their stare-off by looking down at Ben.

Uma cackled. "What are you gonna do, Ben? *Splash me?"*

Mal's eyes sparkled brighter as she hovered beside Ben and glowered at Uma, her dragon wings flaring out in anger.

"That's enough! This isn't the answer! The fighting has got to stop! Everyone!" yelled Ben. He looked at Mal. "Nobody wins this way. We have to listen and respect each other. It won't be easy. But let's be brave enough to try."

Uma rolled her eyes.

Mal's green sparkle faded from hers, and she straightened up a little.

Ben turned to Uma. "Uma, I know you want what

is best for the Isle! Help me make a difference!"
Everyone at the rail of the yacht watched in silence as
Ben held out his hand to Uma.

She looked torn. Her eyes softened. She reached
out a tentacle to Ben, about to touch his hand. Instead,
she dropped his beast-head ring into his hand.

Ben watched her lower silently beneath the waves.
And then Uma was gone.

The crowd aboard the yacht watched Uma head
out to sea, and they exhaled a collective sigh of relief.
The clouds parted, and the sky twinkled with infinite
stars. Ben took his eyes off Uma's wake and swam
back to the boat. Jay and Carlos lowered a ladder, and
a sopping wet Ben climbed up. Everyone cheered for
him. Then Mal flew up and hovered above them.

Mal's wings closed, and then . . .

POOF!

Everyone gasped.

She vanished in a swirl of purple smoke—and
dropped on two feet on the yacht in front of the stained
glass. She was Mal again, but not quite the same Mal.

Her hair was long and thick and purple. She wore
the purple dress depicted in the stained glass, with its

purple cape and rich layers of fabric that swept past her feet. The dress sizzled where it touched the wet deck. Mal patted out the fiery embers, and the crowd giggled. A gold crown shimmered atop her head. She curtsied to Ben, who bowed. Mal grinned and laughed. Fanfare played, and two guards took her by the elbows and escorted her down the stairs as the crowd clapped for her.

Evie met her at the bottom, and Mal grinned.

"I did not know that I could do that," said Mal.

Evie laughed. "Yeah, that makes two of us." She blew out a few more embers on Mal's dress. "Shall we?" asked Evie, extending a hand.

"We shall," Mal declared as she took her friend's hand and walked toward Ben.

Mal walked straight up to Ben and kissed him.

Everyone cheered and applauded.

"Okay, that's enough," said Carlos, which made everyone laugh.

Beast looked on proudly. "How about that boy of ours?" he said to Belle.

"How about his *girlfriend*?" Belle smiled fondly. "We're in good hands."

"I owe you guys a lot," Ben said to the crowd. "If there's anything I can do or if there's anything you need, please—"

"Umm, actually, there is something you can do, Ben," said Evie. "I know a girl who'd really love to come to Auradon. It's Drizella's daughter, Dizzy. She's like a little sister to me and . . ."

Ben nodded. "Then she should come."

"Okay! Okay, great!" said Evie.

Everyone cheered.

"Actually, there's a lot of kids who'd really love it here in Auradon. Kids just like us who also deserve a second chance. Could I maybe get you . . . a list?"

"Yes. Yes! Absolutely!" said Ben. "Please."

Evie beamed as the the crowd clapped.

A guard approached Mal with her spell book. "My lady Mal."

"Yes," she said.

"We found your spell book below deck," he said to her. "Uma had it."

"Oh." Mal took it and examined the cover, with its gold dragon encircled by a ring of Mal's green and purple spray paint. "Thank you. Um . . ." Mal looked long and hard at the old leather book her mother had once used and Mal had been using as of late to put on the whole perfect-princess performance. The act was over. Mal was free to be herself, and Ben would love her for that. "You know, this seems like the kind of thing that belongs in the hands of Fairy Godmother. Fairy Godmother!"

Fairy Godmother stepped between the guard and Ben. "That's me. Excuse me. Thank you."

"This belongs in a museum," said Mal, handing her the book.

"Yes. And I'm going to take it." Fairy Godmother tucked the spell book under her arm and happily vanished into the crowd.

Mal looked at Ben. "I'm not going to be needing it anymore." She moved toward Ben and playfully kicked water back at him.

Ben grinned and kicked water at Mal. She shrieked, delighted, and turned away.

When she turned back to face him, Ben was beaming. Mal took his crown in her hands and angled it crookedly on his head. She pressed her forehead warmly to his.

CHAPTER TWENTY-SEVEN

AND IN TRUE HAPPILY-EVER-AFTER FASHION, WE PARTIED INTO THE NIGHT.

'CAUSE EVERY GOOD STORY ENDS IN A DANCE PARTY, RIGHT?

Before Mal knew it, everybody was splashing water on her and rolling with laughter.

Music began to play, and a feverish merriment broke out on the deck. Drenched, and with water flying, people twirled and boogied. Carlos break-danced in the center of the deck, then hopped up and danced with Jane. Lonnie and Jay took the floor, followed by Evie and Doug, and then Ben and Mal. Everyone crowded them, cheering and splashing them with water. Above, the stars twinkled magically.

Mal had learned in her heart that she was bold, she was brave, and she believed. She was done hiding. She had looked deep inside, and she was going to be herself from now on: part Isle, part Auradon. She thought about *The Lady's Manners* and laughed. That was another book she'd be happy not to open again.

Mal and Ben embraced. Then he slipped his beast-head ring onto her finger. They were ready to face their future—together. They climbed to the top of the staircase overlooking the deck. Fireworks burst overhead. It truly was a happy ending. She turned to face her friends, and she and Ben waved to them.

Mal was lady of the court. She was perfect the way she was. Everyone knew it.

And most important, so did Mal.

EPILOGUE

THERE YOU HAVE IT–THE END OF THE STORY. THE *ACTUAL* HAPPILY EVER AFTER. OR IS IT?

The next day, in Lady Tremaine's Curl Up and Dye salon, Dizzy was sweeping.

The shop was empty. Footsteps sounded. Dizzy looked up to see royal messengers enter, smiling in pale yellow suits. One handed a scroll of paper to her.

Dizzy removed her headphones, took the paper, and unfurled it. The Auradon crest was at the top, and a typed note with two handwritten lines was at the bottom.

Dizzy read it aloud. " 'His Royal Majesty King Ben of Auradon and his councillor Miss Evie of the Isle hereby request the pleasure of your company,

Dizzy Tremaine, for the current academic year at Auradon Prep'!" Her voice grew louder and more excited. " 'Please notify His Majesty's couriers of your response to this request. We'd love you to join us at Auradon Prep. Will you come?' Signed King Ben." Dizzy screamed. She hugged the royal messenger, who beamed. She screamed again. Above, her wicked grandmother banged the floor and shouted, "Knock it off!" Dizzy giggled and smiled. She looked over the scroll of paper again. The messengers turned and marched out.

She ran off to pack.

At long last, Dizzy was going to Auradon.

Not far from the Isle, Uma rose from the waves and looked back at the party boat glowing in the distance. She grinned. "What? You didn't think this was the end of the story, did you?" Uma said. With that, she cackled and lowered back under the water until, with a single ripple, she was gone.

ABOUT THE AUTHOR

ERIC GERON is a writer, editor, singer, and actor. He is best known for writing the *New York Times* best-selling novelization of the film Disney's *Descendants*, under his pen name Rico Green, and editing children's books, most notably *Gravity Falls: Journal 3*. He was raised in Summit, New Jersey, received a degree in creative writing from the University of Miami, and now resides in Los Angeles. You can find him on Facebook, Instagram, and Twitter @EricGeron.

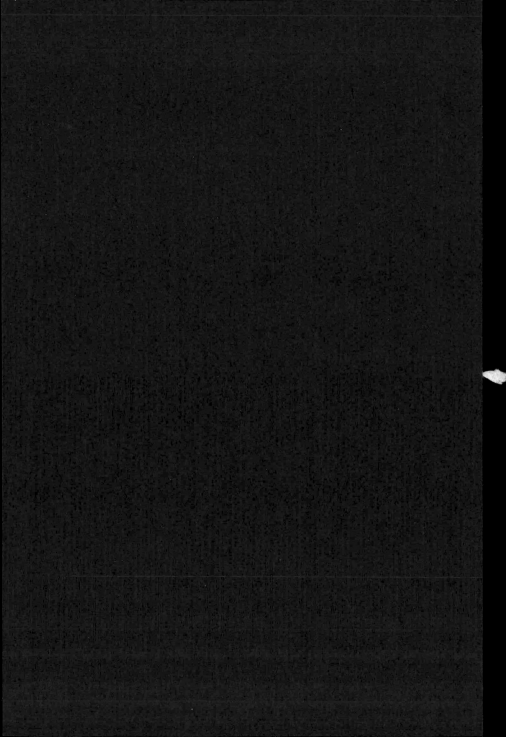